LOW-RISK ACTIVITIES

LOW-RISK ACTIVITIES

STORIES BY

J EFRON

Book Design: Publications Unit, Department of English,
    Illinois State University; Director: Steve Halle, Production
    Assistant: Jalissa Jones
Cover design: Matthew Revert
Typeface: Baskerville

Library of Congress Cataloging-in-Publication Data is
available from the Library of Congress.
ISBN: 978-1-57366-213-0
E-ISBN: 978-1-57366-916-0

CONTENTS

LAN CAIHE

"Tonight's speaker has come here all the way from Fukuoka, Japan. This remarkable person needs no introduction: author of the best-selling memoir, *Lan Caihe, Full of Sex*, please give a heartfelt welcome to Lan Caihe."

"Thank you for having me, Clairent. Am I saying that right, Clairent?"

"Yes, and may I add, that for many of us who have not heard you speak before tonight, your voice oozes elegance."

"Thank you. It may be a blessing from my malformed Adam's apple."

"An *Eve's Apple*."

"Yes, that's what I called it in the book."

"Gorgeous book, by the way. Everyone, you must read it if you haven't. Now Lan, I want to get right into it. For those who have not yet read your memoir, you were abandoned by your Chinese father and Japanese mother because of your sex, but have managed to lead the most incredible life despite this beginning. There is so much in the book, but people have been driven wild by many of the mysteries that have surfaced."

"Is that why this center has sold out?"

"I'm sure that's not why, but your fans are certainly interested. First. Lan Caihe. That is not the name you were given at birth."

"No, it wasn't. But, as I talk about in the first chapter, I don't remember my name, and Lan was a nickname given to me by a Chinese woman at the orphanage."

"Do you really not remember your name? I'm sure a lot of readers wondered about that."

"I like to believe that Lan Caihe *is* my actual name, and that my parents may have gotten it wrong."

(pause for laughter)

"So, a woman called you Lan."

"Yes, and I filled in the *Caihe* later, once I understood why she had used that name."

"Right, so for those of us who don't know, Lan Caihe is one of the eight immortals from Chinese history, and the only one whom historians argue over the sex, many believing that Lan Caihe was dual-sexed."

"That's right. In Japan, where I was born, when a newborn displays both male and female genitalia, a decision is made to *correct* one of the two in an attempt to give the baby a single gender. In my case, my father stole me from the hospital before that decision was made."

"But it wasn't in order to save you, was it."

"No. As I explain, I was abandoned shortly after."

"And how do you know all this?"

"My mother wrote me letters throughout her life, and after tracking her down, I acquired them."

"And how long ago did your mother pass away?"

"You know that is a question I would like to avoid."

"Apologies. But seeing you in person, I cannot believe how young you look."

"My body stopped aging at some point in my twenties."

"How can that be?"

"I don't know."

"Have you consulted any specialists or doctors?"

"I know you've read my book. That is the main reason I fled Japan."

"Right, of course. But since this book has come out, you have been under a lot of scrutiny. Not only because of the questions your book has piqued, but also because of the memoir's timeline and what you say about your body. The public believes you owe it to humanity to cooperate with the scientific community, that there could be breakthroughs in human longevity if . . . "

"If I am telling the truth? I have no desire to become a science experiment so it's better if people don't believe me, isn't it?"

"On behalf of all the readers I have to ask: are you telling the truth?"

"My response would be that my publisher is one of the largest in the world, with a team of scrutinizing fact-checkers. I have provided them with enough details to conduct research that confirms the facts of my life. As part of my contract, these details were made known only for the purpose of confirming the truth of my story. None of it would be included in the memoir, none of it would be revealed by anyone affiliated with the production of the book."

"Why go through such lengths to withhold this information if you have already confirmed that it's true?"

"Psychology. Without the facts in front of them, readers will still doubt the truth of my story. Taking someone's word for it, especially the employees of a publishing company that profits from my story, doesn't satisfy the curiosity, and for that matter doesn't necessarily prove anything in the eyes of the reader. I can tell you it's true and tell you that people vouch for me, but without seeing the proof yourself, there may still be doubt in your mind."

"I'll admit that there is."

"I am hoping that this suspicion will dismiss me somewhat, keep me safe from science experiments and such."

"But you are admitting this now."

"For the same reason, it doesn't matter."

"But there is reference, albeit obscure, to a war Japan was involved in that made life quite dangerous for a while, because, as you write in your book, the legal documents you were using were forged. That had to have been World War Two, as Japan hasn't been engaged in a war for over seventy years."

"Do you believe that?"

"No. Look at you! You're thirty at most, and even *that* would be hard to believe. But still your book has some seemingly impossible inclusions, and as you have said, you have proof somewhere."

"I don't have proof any longer, aside from the proof that I am here in front of you and this book. I destroyed everything, including my mother's letters, to protect myself from people who may be, um, too enthusiastic in trying to solve the mystery of Lan Caihe."

"You must admit the implausibility of your condition."

"Yes, though there are others like me out there."

"Immortals?"

"Completely dual-sexed. I do not believe that I am immortal."

"Let's backtrack a bit, to the orphanage. That's where you learned to read and write."

"Yes, the night nurse spent a lot of her time with me. I don't remember the first couple of years, but based on the accounts of others who worked there, I have that woman to thank for my life today."

"But she is no longer with us, is she."

"No, she died a long time ago."

"About how long ago was that?"

(no answer)

"Right. Moving on. How long were you in the orphanage?"

"Nine years."

"Could you talk a little about that?"

"The orphanage wasn't large, about twenty-five children, almost all of whom had mental or physical disabilities. I fell into neither category and noticed that I was treated differently than the rest of the kids. For one, that nurse I mentioned earlier became, for all intents and purposes, my private tutor and guardian. I didn't understand the dynamics at the time, but she was quite protective of me because of a couple that also worked at the orphanage."

"I don't want to reveal too much of your book, but this woman had reason to distrust that couple, whom you have comically named Bonnie and Clyde in your memoir."

"Yes, well. I may have done that to mitigate the terror I feel when I think about them. It's easier to think about them as robbers than child traffickers."

"Do you know what became of them?"

"No, I never found out. I never wanted to. But for the three months that my tutor/caregiver at the orphanage was away for health issues, those two prepared to have me sold to an underground group in China. This is information I gathered from police reports that the woman looking after me had filed. The two fled the country but that's all I know."

"Do you think about how close your life was to being drastically different?"

"I think about the children they successfully smuggled during their thirteen years at the orphanage, and about how no effort has been made to find or repatriate those taken."

"You are doing something about it now, though."

"Yes, this *star power* has given me a voice. And the proceeds from my book's sales have made me a bit of a lobbyist, vying for children's rights and reform in adoption system's worldwide, to make adoption and easier and safe option."

"Well put. And that is one of the reasons we were so eager to have you speak at our arts and education center. There are so many larger venues that have requested your time, so we thank you for including us on your tour."

"I have built most of my tour around centers like this one. I prefer to speak to smaller crowds and align myself with institutions that have been, as they say, fighting the good fight, for decades. The overhead lighting also tends to be kinder at more intimate venues."

(pause for laughter)

"If you call a four-hundred-seat auditorium and packed standing room, intimate."

"It is a bit though, isn't it? Spaces packed with people were essential to my childhood. Humans generate a surprising amount of energy and I like to think that when our fossil fuels run dry, we can all huddle together and complain in rooms that aren't too big."

"Like communes."

"Without the negative connotation communes tend to have. But I think we could all benefit from living in one. Epicurus created one to great success, though even he had his share of detractors."

"You spent ten years living in one, correct?"

"Yes. I probably still would be if it had not been dismantled."

"We won't spoil that part for our soon-to-be readers."

"Sorry, I don't mean to tease you!"

"Our audience will forgive you, I'm sure. Besides, you have brought a copy of your book and have agreed to read a few select passages for us today."

(pause for applause)

"Would you mind indulging us?"

"Of course, thank you. Allow me to frame the book just a little. I have chosen to write the book as an address to myself. It was a way to abate the pain of writing it, telling it to myself like it was only a story. I also requested that my publisher keep some of the spelling anomalies because I didn't want this book to be perfect, and I didn't want editors changing my language into something cleaner, correcting it, fixing it. Let it be partially broken, I told them."

"Spelling anomalies, I like that phrase. And I was wondering about the decision to leave those in. Thank you for sharing why."

"I would like to start by reading the first two pages."

"Whenever you are ready."

"You are about to die in a pile of sodden leaves and they are in the bedroom *trying* again, their lovemaking full of fear because of the truth you have shown them. When the incision was made and you were pulled headfirst from her abdomen, the doctors remarked on the demiracle of your birth. Then they scratched their heads. Was it how long you were overdue that caused both sex organs to flourish? Your mother has tears of pain and remorse as your father humps against her. He hides his sorrow in the pillow, nearly suffocating from visages of you.

Lan Caihe, in your first decade you a narrowly escape the lion's cager, during the next ten you dangle your legs in. You will fall in and climb your way out. There will follow decades of numbness, one decade of bliss. When others you have loved begin to die you will seriously consider your body's stasis, why the aging process stopped during your third decade, peak fertility.

Lan Caihe, you are and always have been, hairless, right down to your pubic bone. And you have a virile penis and a fertile womb. If the angles were not an impossible you could impregnate yourself and have your own child. This story, these pages, are the consequence of you, each word lain down cementing a structure that can never be demolished. Are you a sure you want to continue?"

"Thank you, Lan Caihe. The first pages are so gripping and leave you wanting so much more. You make a point of showing how difficult it was to write this work. Were there times you were forced to stop?"

"Actually, no. Because of how I framed it, I had some inherent distance. However, I didn't consider what it would be like to be on tour, reading these passages over and over. Writing it down and moving on, you can get closure, move beyond it. Rereading it is much more difficult emotionally."

"I see."

"But there is catharsis through reading as well. Acceptance of the life I have lived. A reminder of ownership. I am happy to be reading for you here today. Allow me to continue from a little later on in the book."

"Yes please."

"To set this part, I should mention that by the time I had become a teenager I'd placed out of the orphanage. I was invited to live with my tutor/caregiver, who I had already viewed as my surrogate mother. I was not adopted, because that, legally in Japan, has other complications, but she took me into her home and homeschooled me because of my anxieties. I continued to live with her for a very long time, through her old age. This section takes place during the twilight of that time. This part is a little graphic. I hope there are no children in the audience. But I wanted to share this particular series of events to show my struggle as a dual-sex person."

"This evening's event is only open to those eighteen years and older. That was how we advertised it and our ticket collectors checked IDs before admittance."

"Like buying a magazine at a drugstore."

"We hope this event has drawn a more sophisticated crowd."

"Only joking. I hope I can meet your expectations."

"Though you live within it, you have always avoided your own body. When puberty's involuntary nighttime ejaculations began you didn't believe when your embarrassment could get worse. Remembering how you tried to clean the sheets so your caregiver wouldn't know seems like stepping into a light dream when compared to the you experiences you have accumulated since.

The man who takes your virginity looks as nervous as you at first. He's a fifty-year-old office and clerk who solicits you at a bar, offering yo money for sex. You are tipsy but still insulted. You have never slapped anyone, never wanting tour attract attention, but you picture the print of your hand and his stung face. You turn away and say no, in that order, so it's possible that he doesn't hear you. He comes around your side and shows you the contents of his moth bursting wallet. He's drunker and saying it's all for you.

More than your anxiety about the morals of your actions, you are concerned with whether he thinks you are a man or a woman. You have dressed in no leading way and your face is left a mystery to all who meet you. You follow him outside thinking, of all the things, *is this man gay?*

He takes you to one of those hourly hotels that wait in the invisible eye of daily commuters, and you are worried when he copays for half a night. In the room, you realize that this is a huge mistake. You begin to make an excuse to leave, which is when hem breaks down at your knees.

"She's humiliated me in front of the whole neighborhood, having sex with a delivery boy. A *boy* practically! How can I be a man in my own house after that!?"

You don't understand exactly what he means but sense that you are being mused for revenge sex. Oddly, this puts you at ease a bit. It's easier to understand his motive and you don't feel as threatened as before.

"I'm not like other people," you say, unsure as to which gender you should affiliate with.

"I don't care," he says, slurring his words enough that you notice it. "I would choose a dog over my cheating wife."

His words hurt, though it clearly isn't his intention. But when he takes out his wallet and stuffs the contents into your hands immediately after saying this, it feels like an apology. You know taking the money (which you are) makes you complicit in the affair. There is at least two hundred thousand yen in your slender hands. You have never touched so much money, unclean crisp bills without even a crease or stain; it makes you wonder who ever thought up the phrase *dirty money*. Not wanting to remind yourself that someone has just bought you, you fold the bills up and slip them into the back pocket of your pants.

It isn't until you underess, slowly removing your shirt to reveal your breasts, seemingly bigger in their nakedness under the after gaze of a stranger, taking your white underwear down last, and your slowly. It's in that slowness you sense something dirty about the previous transaction. You wait for his reaction. His eyes had widened upon seeing those breasts birth, and though the penis and testicles obscure the vagina hidden just a little lower, he doesn't flinch or even show surprise.

He continues to stare at your body along after you have undressed, your skin chilled to goosebumps because of how you bared yourself.

"Will you touch yourself?" he asks. You were not expecting this request. You had an image of sex in the dark, quick and promiscuous. But the lights of the hotel room are not as dark as they should be and he is still fully clothed, complete with tie and couple pocket square.

"How should I do it?" you ask. You are unsure as to of what he expects. Has he seen your vagina? Does he want you to act like a woman more a man? But this is also your first time experimenting with yourself. Aside from bathing and using the bathroom, you have very little to don with what lies beneath your waist.

"You could stroke yourself, rub your nipples." He speaks as though these are suggestions, as though two hundred thousand yen hasn't already turned his words into commands.

You do as he *suggested*, rubbing your fingers across your breasts and taking your phallus into your other, trying to coax an erection. But you can't. You are shivering despite not being cold, shaking under the glare of eyes and lights.

"Can I sit down?" you ask. He nods.

You take a seat near him on the edge of the bed and continue unsuccessfully to rouse yourself.

"I'm sorry," you say afterthought a little while. He takes this as an invitation to help, first assuming command of your penis, then rubbing your balls. You assume he likes this being done to him. After some fondling, he finds, just they below your testicles, the slick slit leading to your clitoris. He works his fingers down father, easing your legs apart, and there is a sensation there unlike his previous pumping. You are wet. Not aroused but wet. You viewed this as a success, that despite your failing penis, he can have sex with you and maybe you and end this mistake quickly.

Before he says anything, you see him lifting your testicles and looking down. He does this abashedly at first, and you lift them yourself so he can see more clearly what he has purchased. You have the simultaneous need for him to be at ease with this, mingled with a slight hope that he will be repulsed but still pay you something for the embarrassment before leaving, so you can escape without having to experience the followed confusion you assume sex will bring.

"You have a pussy," he says.

You nod, unable to speak.

"Can I," he trails off. He has forgotten about the money he has but given you. You look down on the floor and see your pants. The contents of that bulging pocket are the reason you are nodding.

You nod again, still unknowable to speak.

He slides his fingers down over your clitoris and inserts his index finger. Even that feels large. His excitement is evident and though you haven't had any experience with this before you know he is pushing too fast and too hard too soon. He brings his other hand to your penis after a while and, in a strange hunched position revealing a bald patch on the top of his head, he plays with both of your sex organs.

He stops to take his clothes off. You cant tell by his haste that he is both aroused and he embarrassed. His penis is hard and small, but still thick compared to his index finger. He has a round belly, and a small trail of hair below the crevice of his belly button. You focus on this area, too embarrassed to look any higher. He lays you back on the bed and slides himself into you easily. There isn't much pain but it's present, it accompanies the thrusts that push his weight against you. You feel a pressure in your penis as his heft sandwiches it against your stomach.

It doesn't take you long to get used to his motion. Your penis is hard and you come truth on your belly before he does."

"I think I'll stop there."

"And this was your first sexual experience."

"Yes. He took my virginity."

"I don't want to step on the toes of your book too much, but you continued having relations with him, the man you call 'Mr. Salary' in your book."

"Yes. I learned a lot about my body by having sex with him."

"You don't explain this in your book, but is that why you continued to have relations with him?"

"You can say, sex."

(pause for laughter)

"Okay, yes. Sex with him."

"Why. I don't really remember my reasons. Failure to accept myself, to allow myself worth, confused: I suppose these were all wrapped up in it. But I remember liking the fact that he was older and out of shape. That empowered me a bit. I didn't feel like I had to be ashamed of my body if he wasn't ashamed of his. That sounds cruel but it was how I felt. But I also felt secure with him. I know there is a dark side to sex and this was a man whose intentions were quite clear. He continued to pay me and paid handsomely more for certain scenarios I lay out in the book."

"Are you talking about your aborted pregnancy?"

"That, and when he paid me for a sample of my semen. He was more fascinated about how my body worked than I was at the time."

"It must have taken a lot of courage to have sex."

"Why do you say that? Yes, it did."

"You weren't that young when you first had sex. Close readers have noticed the sexual encounter you describe couldn't have happened much earlier than the sixties based on circumstantial descriptions like the 'love hotels' you went to. But other sections in your book hint at events much earlier in history. So, then you were, well—"

"A late bloomer, I believe the saying goes."

"Yes."

"It wasn't my intention to *hint* at events that station me in time. I don't want to create any mystery around my age, but it really would be difficult to write a book that ignores your surroundings."

"Then you are admitting that you have lived through events that took place earlier than the sixties?"

"Clairent, you invited me here to read and have a conversation. There is no need for confessions or admissions when two people are having a conversation."

"I apologize. Like so many others, I feel really invested in your story. And of course, I'm curious."

"I'm sure sleuthing readers have found hints or even facts that lead one to place my life on a timeline, even though I tried to avoid this as much as possible. The real reason I wrote the book, and the reason why I tried to keep the timeline obscure, are actually the same."

"Considering how much you seem to value your privacy, there must have been a very good reason to write a book that would gain international attention and have people scrutinizing your life."

"Would you believe that I wanted to chronicle my life?"

"No, I wouldn't. For that you could have just written a diary."

"True."

"Then you wanted people to read it."

"I wanted *someone* to read it. Let's leave it at that."

"I can't possibly! You had a particular audience in mind. A particular person? Liza from your time spent in the commune?"

(Lan Caihe covers the mic and whispers something to Clairent).

"Everyone, you'll have to forgive me for not answering that last question. Allow me to atone with another passage from the book."

"Yes, please. I'm sure we are all eager to hear more."

"The last passage I will read is from a section outlining how I got to America. For those of you who haven't read the book, I fled to America due to an interest the Japanese government had begun taking in me. The section is obviously before the years I spent on a commune here in America, which Clairent has just alluded to. I think this section is appropriate, as I am speaking to you in the city I first lived in when I got to the states."

"Which should have been quite difficult as you couldn't even prove your age!"

"Nor did I want to."

"Paying off the dockworker-people was not a problem, nor was bribing the two deckhands who found a relatively spacious storage closet for you to stow away in. Your English is bad and it makes you feel less want than them but they don't seem to care because you have offered them quite a substantial sum, nearly half of the money you had kept saved from Mr. Salary [name for your sexual partner of nearly ten years]. You are leery of the way they look at your breasts, even after they have them money in their hands. You remind them of the money in their hands but you think they worst. It can't be helped based on your experiences. They will sell you to other sailors, bloodletting other men on board know where you are holed up, for a price. But you thank them. You *thank them*, despite these fears. And because of these fears, you immediately leave your accommodations once they have left you alone. The freighter is the size of a small town, with levels and levels of containers. There is a level of freezer storage, living quarters, mazes containing the ship's inner workings, cramped bathrooms on various levels, and an upper deck that you are too afraid to visit.

When the engine of the ship begins to roar, you are exploring one of the lower levels. Checking to ensure no light leaks from beneath any door of a room you are about to enter, you push open heavy metal doors to a variety of storage areas. You settle on a room that contains bags and bags of rice. After moving all of the bags a meter or so forward, you have a small area to sleep behind them. This serves to create a barrier between you and anyone entering the room that they likely won't notice. The only problem you potentially face is not knowing how many bags they go through in one voyage, which would possibly expose your makeshift hideaway.

When you get further out to sea, your stomach churns. Rough weather makes your time spent in your small bunk unbearable. You feel sick but the smell of vomit would smother the rice-filled storeroom and you can't risk being exposed. Traveling to the bathroom every time nausea reared would increase the chances of being found. Nor it is possible to purge in an adjacent room, for the smell would raise suspicions. There is only one recourse left to you and it is foul. You have been spared having to choke on the cocks of dirty sailors, and this knowledge somehow makes it a little easier to swallow the vomit that continually rises up in your mouth. There are times, however, when the need to vomit happens faster than you can clamp your mouth and spurts of puke spill out between your lips and onto the floor. To clean this slippage and purify the air, you tear open one bag of rice. It is the bag you have been using as a pillow at night. You spill grains of rice onto the places vomit has landed on the floor. They work well at suppressing the smell and soak up the vomit after a while. During times when you are feeling better you search out half-finished water bottles and rags or clothes that have been left in different parts of the lower depths of the ship. You use these rags to clean up the puke-soaked rice and dispose of them near the furnace area of the ship where the smell of oil is so strong that nothing else can be smelled over it. The water is mainly to quench your bloodthirst, which is always constant, but you occasionally waste it to wash the floor where you sleep.

Tracking time in your windowless stockroom is impossible, but since your stomach and legs become so used to the undulations of the tanker that you no longer feel the movement, you assume that weeks have passed. Your appetite returns and during times when it is impossible to steal food from the kitchen's storage, you munch on uncooked kernels of rice pillaged from your dwindling pillow. As far as safety is concerned, the rice bags aren't depleting from the storeroom as fast as you'd feared. There is the infrequent, solitary man who enters the room to grab a new bag. He does this quickly.

One evening, when your period is severe and rats come sniffing around, chatting in their little voices and nibbling the rucksack pants you fashioned for yourself, in desperate need of a change of clothes because you have started to notice your own smell, you hear voices. The rats cease their chatter and listen to the voices echoing off of the metal walls in the hallway outside your storeroom. You hear them opening a door to a room close to yours, then then another even closer. They talk intermittently in awe language you don't understand, but the impatience of their voices requires no translation. They are looking for something.

When they open the door to your room, you are afraid they will smell you, smell your blood, smell your dried vomit, and smell the clothes you have left out to dry after having tried to wash them unsuccessfully in the bathroom. They are in and shout quickly, slamming the door. They follow the same pattern all the away down the hallway. You try to remember what the voices of the two men you bribed resound like but are unable to. The transaction had been hurried to keep you hidden, and you were so worried about them staring at your body that their voices were moistly lost. You think it must be the same bought-men, looking form you. How long will they keep up they search? Have they been searching the entire time you've been away at sea?

You have gotten used to the gnawing hunger and meager portions of mainly uncooked grains, you have settled into the habit of long swaths of sleep because the dark of this room allows room for little else other than sleep and imagining the world outside. You have gotten used to the metal floor, come to love the rice sack you use as a pillow, and even the recent addition of citizen-mice in your hideout. They give you much needed confidants, and at times you believe you are whispering their language. It's crazy to think of them as kinship; your thoughts drift to your caretaker, who you buried yourself because she told you not to use the money you had been saving on a funeral. She knew you would need that money should you have to leave Japan. She seemed to know that time would come. She knew your secrets. It was she who you confided in when that government friend of Mr. Salary began questioning you in public. Your skin carries the only visible memory of her in the form of a snake bite. You were still quite young and stupidly barefoot in long grass. She cut across the fang marks with a knife and sucked out blood and venom. You wonder if you could have died from this, if you could die at all.

Malnutrition and the fevers that sometimes result have become dull with pains on a voyage that seems like an endless purgatory. There are times when you are brave enough to search out the kitchen's storage. But since the recent search of your room by those two men, you are much more cautious and go hungry more often than not. Even in the worst straits of hunger, you fear those men above it all else."

"Wow, that must have been a harrowing passage. And for those of us who have read the book, we know that it gets worse before the journey ends."

"Yes, but I'm quite lucky actually when you consider how much worse it could have been."

"And compared to this voyage, your entry into America was rather uneventful. Or else you chose not to write about the bureaucracy of your entry."

"I thought it best to spare the readers the boredom of getting all of my paperwork in order."

"I find it quite remarkable that you were able to emigrate without being deported. The US government is pretty notorious with immigrants. Any secrets you would like to share with those who want to do the same?"

"I wish I could help but I just seemed to have slipped through the cracks of the US Immigration System."

"Our government is pretty notorious for that as well! I want to thank you so much for agreeing to read and speak with us here today. It has been a real pleasure. You were also kind enough to extend an invitation to our audience members for a question and answer section, which I would like to add you have not allowed at many of your venues for some fairly obvious reasons. Before we get started, I would like to remind the audience of the nondisclosure agreements you signed as well as the consent forms acknowledging that questions should be asked respectfully, not intrusively, and above all if there are any questions Lan doesn't feel like answering for any reason, Lan can pass on them. Shall we begin?"

"Hi, Lan. Molly here. I loved your book. I'm studying Japanese and I love languages and your writing is really interesting to me. I'm actually going to write my undergraduate thesis on your book! You have been translated into seven different languages already, Japanese among them. Why did you decide to write this book in English as opposed to Japanese?"

"I appreciate the enthusiasm for my writing, thank you. As you probably know from my book, I've been living in the United States for quite a number of years now and it just felt more natural to be writing in the language I'm surrounded by every day."

"My question is for Clairent actually. After Lan Caihe whispered to you, you looked a bit scared. What did Lan say to you?"

"I apologize, but that is something we cannot discuss. Unless Lan would like to add something, we will move on to the next question. Sorry!"

"Regarding something you talked about at the end of the interview, I wanted to ask if Lan is in this country illegally. I don't mean that disrespectfully but it took me nearly eight years to get citizenship here and am stunned by how fast it seemed you were able to obtain documentation allowing you to stay."

"I assure you it was not easy."

"But didn't you get permission to work rather quickly, or did I read that wrong?"

"When I received my documentation to work here, the United States was much more welcoming to immigrants. But I was still required to provide some background information that was quite difficult to prove. But I think one of the reasons the process went quicker was because there wasn't the same animosity as we have seen in the post-two-thousand world."

"Thank you. I'm sorry, but, it's just that, the way your writing portrays your entry and first few months in America, it just lacked that fear that so many of us live with, made to feel like we are stealing something every day just being here."

(Questioner tears up.)

"Questioner, what is your name?"

"Maite."

(Long pause.)

"Maite. I'm going to tell you something, and this is why everyone here has signed the NDA. I don't want to lie to you and make you think that my entry and first years spent here was like the uncertainty and fear you must have felt. Truthfully, I didn't have to suffer that. I will not go into the details, and it isn't anywhere in my book, but I did sacrifice something akin to my morality to obtain legal documentation. It was not sexual, and I don't think something like that would have managed to cross the massive barriers I faced without even a birth certificate to my name, not even my name but a name stolen from a goddess. I can't sit here and pretend that my journey through this country could compare to yours. Yes, the things printed in the book are true, on that I give my word. But there are things that I left out, and this particular detail is the source of much shame and I can't talk about it even if I wanted to. I just want you to know that, Maite."

"Thank you."

"I have read your book a dozen times now, Lan. Probably more."

"Why, thank you!"

"And I've been waiting for an opportunity to hear you read from your book. I have to say the five-hour trip was definitely worth it."

"Five hours. I'm impressed."

"Listening to you today, I noticed that you faithfully read

the book, *spelling anomalies* and all. I was even able to catch some that I had missed."

"Even after fourteen reads? I don't think my editors even gave me that much time!"

"It was interesting to hear your reasons for why you chose to keep those in the book, but I have a theory that the anomalies are deliberate."

"Well, I deliberately wanted to remain true to my writing and editing abilities."

"I noticed a couple of patterns with the anomalies though. As far as I can tell they are always additions to the text, meaning if they are taken away the text reads without grammatical or spelling errors. They are never a case of mistaking an 'a' for and 'e,' for example. On the first page, which was the first passage you read tonight, the anomalies were quite easy to find. You added 'de' to 'miracle', 'a' before 'narrowly', 'r' to the word 'cage', 'an' before the word 'impossible', and 'a' before 'sure.' These aren't usual spelling errors. And I found an odd 'yo' that looks like something was forgotten until you see the next inclusion, 'tour', which makes 'your' when omitted correctly. And there are some questionable word choices like 'bought' and 'truth' that seem to be purposeful."

"I'm sorry to interrupt you, questioner, but I believe that we touched upon this during the interview. If you don't have a specific question, there are others waiting to be called upon."

"Well, Clairent, I think there's more to this than the quirks of a non-native writer, and though I haven't been able to find all of them, the message is becoming clear."

"Message?"

"In the second section you wrote, dockworker-*people*, why? When you read out loud tonight, I heard things like '*your* sex' and '*left* a mystery," words I wasn't sure were necessary. Like I mentioned earlier, many of the clues have been difficult to find."

"I think it would be better if we moved on to the next questioner, Clairent."

"Wait! I'm here on behalf of an interested party."

"You may leave now. Clairent, you may call on the next person."

"I don't work for the government, if that's what you are worried about!"

"I'm not worried about that."

"I believe Lan asked for the next questioner. Let's respect Lan's wishes."

"Just listen. He's prepared to pay you a fortune. You or your *daughter*. That's who this book is for, isn't it?"

"I have nothing to say to you. Please leave."

(audience murmuring)

"Is what he says true, Lan? What leads him to believe you have a daughter?"

"I thought there might be someone out there who would find comfort in my words. Honestly, I don't know if there is anyone out there like me. Selfishly, I like to think that I'm not alone even though I know the extent of what that would mean. I hope that if someone picks up my book today, or tomorrow, in thirty years or in eighty-seven, that they will be able to find me through my writing, or at least know that they are not alone. Sorry, I know there are people with questions."

JIMMY ONLY

The **MP Psychological Evaluation** is a requisite part of your application. Much like the **Classified Information Nondisclosure Agreement** form that has already been signed and submitted, this battery exam is a necessary component in determining whether or not you will be selected for the position. As such, it behooves the applicant to complete this test with unreserved honesty. A nontransparent scoring rubric has been devised for assessing this test (meaning: do not assume the perceived *correct* answer to any one question). The correct answer may not be the altruistic choice, and vice versa. Do not assume we are *looking* for any particular answer. As this test will be used as a window into your ability to handle the job for which you are applying, please take the time to consider the mental repercussions and consequential long-lasting damage that answering falsely might incur if you were to be selected.

Take as long as is necessary to answer the following questions. Answers are selected by circling one of the choices (which are indicated by the bolded font within each question). Circling multiple answers will always be viewed as an invalid response. Not circling any choice will affect your score.

Ex. Which color makes you think of spring, **yellow** or **green**? (**Yellow** has been selected.)

Section 1: Situations

1) Which would you rather lose, **both thumbs** or your **sense of right and wrong**?

2) Which would you rather lose, **both thumbs**, or your **sense of sight**?

3) Choose which to lose, your **sense of right and wrong**, or your **sense of sight**?

4) What percent of people do you think would use a 1/2 million dollars selfishly?

   1% 2% 5% 10% 20% 50% 60% 70% 80% 90% 95% 100%

5) **A million dollars for you** OR **1/2 a million each for 5 people** randomly selected across the world, same conditions as above apply. There are billions of people in the world at this point, 80% of whom are living in poverty. This is only a statistic to keep in mind when considering the 5 people who would randomly receive this money. This is not to imply a correct answer, only food for thought. Do not ever assume transparency as to the *preferred* answer. The information is to be used as an aid in order to entice the applicant into making a thoroughly thought through decision.

6) Which of these sounds most like you: When I'm cold,

   I put on more clothes.   I use a heating device.
   I build a fire.   I remain cold.

7) ~~My wife is a photographer. She had a darkroom in our San Francisco home and she spent so much time there we used to joke about her boycotting the sun. We have since moved, albeit temporarily, and have built a second darkroom, but the atmosphere is incomparable. I can't adequately explain the difference between the two darks (as I have been in both rooms), but this~~

~~new room is unsettling. It could just be that my con-~~
~~cept of darkness has since shifted.~~ **information bias**
Which option do you think is the most effective form of
nonviolent protest?

**hunger strike   silent protest
economic/political noncooperation**

Section 2: Scenarios

Take the people we regard as the most prominent in all dis-
ciplines, the Albert Einsteins, the Pearl Bucks, the Ghandis,
the Cleopatras, the Alexander the Greats, the Confuciuses,
the Beethovens, the Rosalind Franklins, the Sun Tzus, the
Van Goghs, the Jacque Cousteaus, the Miyamoto Musashis
(legendary Buddhist swordsman who wrote a treatise on the
Zen of Decapitation), the Marie Curies, the Edwin Hubbles,
etc., throughout all history and let's assume all of the collective
knowledge has mystically been collected into a pill and ingested
by every living human being, giving everyone the same amount
of nearly endless information regarding everything humans
have learned and discovered (this being limited to knowledge/
information alone—not necessarily will, compassion, etc.).

1)   As a result, would there be **more peace** or **more war/
     conflict?**

2)   Would you want to take this pill? **yes   no**

3)   Do you believe that everyone should have access to this
     pill? **yes   no**

4)   Would you be worried if every person on Earth had this
     kind of power? **yes   no**

5)   ~~There are those of us who can see the future, not because~~
     ~~we are fortune tellers or minor-prophets but because the~~

~~future has already happened and it continues to happen.
If the past often repeats itself, as we've witnessed over mil-
lennia of not learning from our mistakes, then the future,
too, must also repeat itself (as the future will eventually be
in the past), which gives credence to the maxim, "history
repeats itself." And so I can see, before it even happens,
that I will live a long life, because you who are applying
have worked hard to be the best and brightest in your
fields; I have seen your resumes, and have faith in the people we already have on board that our "way of life" (by
which I don't know what I mean) will continue. And this
of course includes the completion of what we here have
already begun work on, something that everyone here
in our makeshift community knows about, regardless of
clearance level, regardless of whether or not they moved
here for their husband's job and have chosen to "live in
the dark" literally and not in any way metaphorically.~~ **IB**
—— I believe that humans should have free will so long as
this will doesn't harm or impede others' free will. If a person, thinking clearly and rationally, was attempting to kill
~~herself~~ **IB** themself, would you try to 'save' ~~her~~ **IB** them?

yes   no

6–10) If women could give birth without the aid of men or
their sperm and it became a normalized part of human culture to an extent where it became the dominant
source of childbirth, and on top of that a woman was
free to choose the baby's biological sex, circle whether
you believe the following would increase ($\uparrow$), decrease
($\downarrow$), or remain unaffected (——):

male population	↑	↓	—
world population	↑	↓	—
War	↑	↓	—
matriarchal societies	↑	↓	—
What biological sex would you choose for a baby (you are limited to only one child and must have one)?	**male**	**female**	**don't care**

Section 3: Short responses

1) Do you believe that silence is a form of violent protest? **yes no**

2) Do you believe that death should be inevitable? **yes no**

3) Do you believe that faith in God(s) and faith in religion is more or less the same thing? **yes no**

4) Where you live, do you lock your doors? **yes no**

5) Are you friends with your neighbors? **yes no**

6) If you could see your entire future would you feel the need to keep living your life if you knew there would be no way to alter the course it would take? **yes no**

7) To ask the previous question a bit differently: From this point in your life, if it meant everything would be the same and you would have all of your memories, would you want to live your life thus far again? **yes no**

8) When you read the word *mine*, what do you think of (closest answer)? **not yours   deep cavity   type of bomb**

9) ~~Lately I've been thinking about hunger, about what it's like to feel, not hungry, but *hunger*. My wife hasn't been eating much, says she hasn't had an appetite. And it could be that there is something much bigger "nourishing" her. She quells her being hungry with some greater clandestine *hunger*. I have asked her quite bluntly if she wishes we weren't married, if she wants me to change my occupation. To both she answered definitively, "no." I believe her, but it doesn't help to diminish the small guilt nestled inside of me. It's combated daily and easily quashed by the excitement of invention and the importance of what we are engaged in. But Eva, though diminished, stabs me with something unspoken. Am I feeling her *hunger*? We have evolved to feel our own emotions, hunger, and pain.~~ **IB** Do you think it would be a beneficial evolutionary trait to be able to feel someone else's emotions, hunger, or pain? **yes no**

10) Do you ever look at others and wish to be them, wonder what it might be like to be them, because you believe yourself to be so much different than them that you couldn't possibly imagine how they think or feel or act? **yes no**

11) Can you imagine nothing? **yes no**

12) Have you ever let someone use a cup or dish that you either knew was unclean or were unsure about? **yes no**

13) What do you believe is a harder substance, **tooth** or **bone**?

14) Do you believe that humans would cooperate more as a species if we had predators? **yes no**

Section 4: Scales

Studies have been conducted that show rating scales such

as these are completed quicker and with less thought than full-sentence questioning. This information is being provided as a reminder to continue with slow thoughtful deliberation before answering each individual question within each grouping.

On a scale from *1–5, 1 being easily imagined* and *5 being impossible to imagine*, please evaluate the following statement: How difficult is it for you to imagine the sound of

a gun being fired	1	2	3	4	5
a dust mote collecting on a lamp	1	2	3	4	5
a powerline snapping	1	2	3	4	5
blinking	1	2	3	4	5
tying your shoes	1	2	3	4	5
~~your wife's hunger~~ IB the moment of death	1	2	3	4	5
a giraffe's call	1	2	3	4	5
snow falling on dead leaves	1	2	3	4	5
a wave crashing (while being under water)	1	2	3	4	5
oil and vinegar separating	1	2	3	4	5

On a scale from *1–5, 1 being not scared* and *5 being terrified*, please evaluate the following:

spiders	1	2	3	4	5
the dark	1	2	3	4	5
cancer	1	2	3	4	5
speaking in public	1	2	3	4	5
~~the person you love most dying~~ **IB** rejection	1	2	3	4	5
your death	1	2	3	4	5
doing nothing with your life	1	2	3	4	5
heights	1	2	3	4	5
bombs	1	2	3	4	5

Which can we do without? Please evaluate the following word-pairs and circle which of the two you believe humanity would be best off without (please take your time and consider how the lack of each choice within the pairs would impact human society).

1	transportation	friendship
2	flowers	basic human rights
3	country borders	over population
4	industrialization	religious buildings
5	clocks, calendars	myths, folktales, etc.

6	possessions	dreams
7	cities	towns
8	instinct	memory
9	pesticides	plastics
10	feeling of love	medicine

The following chart contains words and symbols. Using the leftmost box as your reference, identify (using the choices to the right) what you believe to be the closest available meaning for the contents of the leftmost box in that row.

Ex.

☺	**Happy**	**sad**	**confused**

Ψ	**a bird's footprint**	**a cup**	**a trident**
‼ (as opposed to seeing just "!")	**anger**	**excitment**	**surprise**
☠	**death**	**pirates**	**poison**
which symbol best describes life	♉	♀	⚲
☉	**earth**	**moon**	**sun**
~~The United States of America~~		**information**	**bias**
snow lion	**clarity**	**fearlessness**	**joy**
fish swimming	♒	♋	♓
end of winter	♊	♍	♓	♐
fire	☷	☵	☳	☶

Weigh the word-triplets in order of importance, writing 1, 2, and 3 in the boxes below, 1 being most important.

1)   curiosity ☐   study ☐   reflection ☐

---

2)   As it relates to where we live:

neighbors/community ☐   the domicile itself☐   scenery/
location☐

Preservation of:

1)   your family☐   human beings☐   natural world☐

Section 5: ~~Sickness~~ **information bias**

1)   Given we can cure only one, what should we cure?

    desire   hatred   ignorance

2)   ~~Eva often listened to an hour-long radio program featuring a twenty-minute segment where an artist or critic attempted to describe a work of art as accurately as possible. The segment was started for the benefit of listeners who might not ever see the works themselves but became increasingly popular because of how difficult it was for the artists and critics to accurately describe a painting. We don't get reception for that program in New Mexico.~~

~~When describing Edvard Munch's *The Scream*, one critic couldn't help saying, "we can feel his anguish" and "the soul within is shivering." But these phrases describe what's at the core of the painting and how the critic wants us to feel about it. The few artists and critics who completed a description without these emotional inclusions had a hard time ending the dialogue, as if to try and intimate that what they had described was incomplete. Some critics included the artist's motivation for the particular piece or even biographical information, though some of history's greatest musicians, novelists, painters, etc. refuse to explain~~

~~their work.~~ **information bias**

Does knowing the artist's intention behind the work *limit* how the audience interprets it?

yes no

Section 6: Self-Identity

1) How do you identify yourself? **how I think** or **what I look like**.

2) Which would you say you identify more as being *you*, the *you*:

   that you believe yourself to be.

   that others see and interact with.

3) With the body and mind functioning properly, a human can live for a long time. Do you think human aesthetics such as beauty play a role in this? **yes   no**

4) Language creates our identity. It is not a tool for us to use, but a lens through which our worldview is shaped. From identifying color, sound description, whether or not plural or singular forms exist or even whether or not masculine and feminine notions of words exist, the language we grow with is a box shaping us. Which do you think language is doing more to people,

   connecting the world or **perpetuating cultural separation**?

5) ~~I'm sensing things I can't define. The excitement of our work is different lately. Because of some specific progress everything has become more real. I realize this is not unlike the difference I felt between the two darks of Eva's photo-developing rooms. I want to talk about it but I don't know how so I began talking to myself in the absence of~~

~~Eva's companionship in an attempt to give words to the feelings, which resulted in the following revelation: talking to oneself amplifies the solitary state of the individual in a way that silence never can. When I think about the transition from silence to speaking to myself, I go from nothingness (meaning not necessarily thinking about my existence or humanness) to a lone being creating language for no one else to hear. I become acutely aware of my own isolation because humans inherently know that language is created for others to hear.~~

Do you talk to yourself regularly? **yes no IB**

6) How many conscious thoughts are you capable of having at one time?

   one two three more

7) How difficult was it to answer the last question?

   very somewhat not at all

8) Our senses perceive an uncountable amount of data every second because they are always working. How do you believe a state of sensory deprivation (the ability to remove all of your senses) would affect your consciousness? What do you believe it would feel like?

   **sleep during a non-dream state   death
   being knocked unconscious**

Section 7: Sharks

Sharks have all the senses we have, plus two more we don't: the ability to sense vibration and the sense of electricity. A shark's sense of smell is so sharp that it can detect one drop of blood in a million droplets of water, which depending on where you are from is twenty-five gallons or one hundred liters, and it can smell blood a quarter of a mile away, or about four hundred meters. They also have the ability to see color, coupled with a strong sensitivity to light allowing them to notice very small differences in its intensity. With regard to vibrations, sharks can sense the movement of other animals in the water because of a system of fluid-filled vessels that run the length of their body. They are also capable of sensing electricity, which is emitted in small amounts by all living animals. They are more adept at this than any other animal.

1) What does it feel like to sense electricity? It's like:

   smell   balance   hunger   touch

2) Do you believe that you are more intelligent than a shark?

   yes   no

3) Of the following four options, which do you think is the number one reason people kill each other?

   necessity   desire   hatred   ignorance

4) Do you believe that collectively, humans are more intelligent than sharks? **yes no**

5) Of the following four options, which do you think is the number one reason people kill non-human organisms?

   necessity   desire   hatred   ignorance

6) Approximately what percent of humans do you believe are more intelligent than sharks?

   1% 2% 5% 10% 20% 50% 60% 70% 80% 90% 95% 100%

7) Of the following four options, which do you think is the number one reason sharks kill other organisms?

   necessity   desire   hatred   ignorance

8) Which of these words most closely describes how you view intelligence?

   compassion   harmony   knowledge   nirvana

9) Do you believe yourself to be capable of killing someone for a reason other than utter necessity (if you even believe you can kill out of necessity)? **yes no**

10) What percent of humans do you believe are capable of killing for a reason other than utter necessity, ~~for instance, neglect?~~ **information bias**

    1% 2% 5% 10% 20% 50% 60% 70% 80% 90% 95% 100%

11) ~~Eva told me, in a rare eclipse of conversation that even if I quit my job, it wouldn't change her *conviction*. I tried to ask about that word, fearing its implication. She shakily held a glass of water and braced an arm on the counter for support. I know she isn't doing this *to* me, and I understand that my inability to change her mind mirrors her own inability to stop something much larger. But it doesn't quiet my anger and desperation; I want to ask Eva:~~ **IB** Could you die right now without wishing for a single other thing to have happened in your life? **yes no**

Section 8: Swan Song

Thank you for taking the **Manhattan Project Psychological Examination**. The information will be scored, analyzed, and an evaluation will be mailed back to you in the coming months. If you wish to withdraw your application from the pool at any time, please contact Dr. Fermi in F-Division directly or send correspondence through Dr. Oppenheimer's University of California campus address. The awesome responsibility of ~~building something for the sole purpose of destroying it~~ **IB** developing something to end the war may fall on you.

Part A. This final section presents the examinee with pairings by which circling one of the two bolded pairings will indicate which you choose to continue living, ~~which also highlights my own irreconcilable dilemma~~ **IB**:

1) **the person you love the most**   **everyone on a crowded train**
2) **the person you love the most**   **every other person on earth**

Part B. This subsection will examine the same sets of pairings but in this instance, by circling a choice you will be killing (~~this wording more accurately reflecting my strife~~) **IB** those within the circle:

1) **the person you love the most   every person on a crowded train**
2) **the person you love the most   every other human life on earth**

Once again, I'd like to thank you for enduring the rigorous application process and for your commitment to the preservation of our democracy.   Jimmy Only 1942

*note on the test: I created this test with preliminary assistance from the University of California's Psychology Department. The test was then assessed by Dr. Oppenheimer and edited for **information bias** on the grounds of it being potentially unpatriotic or containing superfluous information. I don't believe myself to be unpatriotic; that being said I have made the decision to administer this test with the stricken questions still included. I hope Dr. Oppenheimer will forgive the inclusion of references to my wife's *hunger strike* (my words, not hers), but applicants should consider not only the global impact of their work, but the potential for more intimate tremors as a result of this work. Feel free to answer these stricken questions in any way you see applicable. They will be scored if answered.

**All applicants who take this test will have the opportunity to receive their results, should they desire to see their aptitude for such a project.

A note to future test-takers who wish to know how they fare psychologically: visit www.jesseefron.com for more information. Look for **MP PSYCH TEST.

SONNY

I wait in a purposely guestless hotel in a room annexed from the lobby. It's a waiting room but includes a four-poster bed amongst pairs of faux-leather chairs and a stray single chair. The room is adorned with ferns of Triassic size in massive antique red-clay pots that also shade the deep purple rugs from the soft thousands of starlike LEDs sunk into the ceiling like a sieve filtering a singular monstrous light source down to bottle-caps of illumination. A living wall overlooks the bed and the pillows are visibly plumped under cloud-plush comforters to insinuate that anyone using the bed should be looking up at the choir of heart-shaped ivy, small black-stemmed ferns, ZZ plants, and others I don't know the names for.

Ah, but what am I doing here, at a private hotel where the eccentric man who owns it keeps a skeleton staff and a solitary concierge with no plans of admitting guests?

"I work for a charity organization that creates infrastructure for equanimity in Mumbai." That's the official spiel. I'm here because of my agreeable face, placid demeanor, and because I am a product of charity, a success story of the thing I'm selling. We rely mainly on donations and the man I am to visit, whom everyone calls Sonny, whom I am under no circumstances to call Sonny, is a man of extraordinary wealth. He is known in our sphere as one of our *pockets* for how reliably he supports our causes.

Call it overreliance, but the charity has stopped its metaphorical marching, neglecting the proverbial door-to-door tromps for small donations, which do end up totaling a healthy sum, surfeited as we have been by whale donations from legacy individuals. And suddenly we find ourselves scrambling, like that grasshopper in the parable with the ants who does nothing to prepare from winter. A couple of the sizable donors have moved onto other whims; with our philanthropy already on their list of accolades, they search for more *fashionable* charities, and we must rely even more on the few *pockets* who actually want to see the city they live in become a city for everyone. Sonny is one such man, though there have been stirrings in popular circles that he has gone mad.

I sit in the single onlooking chair, staring at a queen-size bed, ivory bedding contrasted by a dark wooden headboard with a Latin phrase I don't understand carved into it; I wonder if the hovering rumors might have shadows of truth.

I am escorted into the elevator by a young man dressed in all white like a chef. He pushes the button for the sixteenth floor and we are whisked up quickly and silently. The elevator has no walls, being completely round, and the doors open both in front of and in back of me like two sets of jaws.

I can see that we are in a large bright room, with one exaggeratedly long and rectangular sofa the color of antique red-clay pots, dividing the front of the room that looks out over two-story windows down onto the city. I haven't mentioned this, but it is the middle of the night, 11 p.m. to be exact, and the city lights twinkle to death and back in the smog. There are only a few buildings higher than this one in the vicinity, and they are too far away to see inside. Sonny stands at what appears to be an island in front of a stainless bronze kitchen. Leaving the elevator, I realize that it has deposited us in the center of this echoic studio apartment. There is a ladder that leads off to an open second floor that divides the two-story windows on the right side. The kitchen is separate from everything else and the area immediately to the left of the elevator has a treadmill sunken into the floor that's as wide as the moving walkways you'd see at airports. And beyond that, along the wall adjacent the windows, almost purposefully opposite the kitchen, is a trio of Coca-Cola vending machines.

The young chef announces me, not by name, but generally announces that a guest has arrived, and takes his place behind the island, taking out ingredients without any instruction.

"Please, stand with me," Sonny says.

"It is an honor to meet you, sir," I say. He is dressed in a pinstripe shirt, and his Bollywoodesque handsomeness nearly make his skin glow.

"I've got a problem here. No, not a problem per se, but a challenge. I'm just in the middle of it now. It'll be good to get your opinion."

He was talking to me and he wasn't. He made eye contact like how one can choose to focus on window glass or see right through it.

"It's almost as—"

Sonny's words are interrupted by the whirring of a blender. The chef, he actually is a chef, is shaving coconut into fingernail ribbons while a bluish mixture churns behind blender glass.

I completely miss what Sonny has said, but he doesn't seem to mind.

"Was lacking. But that's precisely it; it's cars at first, right? And then something more exclusive: singular items like pieces of art, especially if the artist is dead and can't produce more. Anyway, you see what I'm getting at."

I nod.

"Right! Experiences. You can't buy those, not the ones I'm talking about. Take for instance this trip I took to Japan last year, that's probably when I first started thinking seriously about this challenge of mine. I was on vacation with my wife, still married I feel I should say, and our helicopter pilot dropped us off in this little town, same name as the dance, the *Tango*, pronounced like, *ankh*, not *mango*."

I contemplate the odd choice to compare the *a* sound with the word, *ankh*. But then Sonny nods above the chef's head and there is an ankh, along with other hieroglyphs etched into the bronze framing above the upper kitchen cabinets.

"Says *rule your time* in Ancient Egyptian."

I don't know what to say.

"You see, we were staying in this villa in the smack-dab center of the village, and there were fishermen out along the shores, and people drying seaweed on handmade racks, children walking to school in neat single file rows with the eldest leading the way and holding a flag like a tour guide, all of them donning bright yellow caps. I saw all this the following morning when I took a walk before breakfast. My wife slept in, on account of her medication. So, as I made my way along the coast, I looked down over the waist-high seawall to get a better look at the sea. The water was perfectly translucent and I could see that the shore was entirely rock, maybe volcanic—I was told Japan has a lot of volcanos, or it did, but there was a little old lady wading through the water with a wooden basket on her back, picking seaweed out of the water. So tiny and small she was I mistook her for a child who had decided to skip school and play in the water. She stooped. She was shrunken. I thought she must have been at least ninety. Possessed by some curiosity I asked if I could join her."

"You speak Japanese?" I ask without thinking.

"No. My interpreter was with me on the walk," he said. His tone shifting to that of someone forced to slow down in traffic.

"I hopped right into the water and began picking seaweed with her, shoes jeans and all. She fussed over my clothes, but I was happy to ruin them in order to help her gather seaweed. She shared some with me afterward as well. If I'm ever back in Tango, I'll pay her a visit. She asked me to come back and do so."

He continues to talk about how it was precisely *that* experience, or that type of experience that preoccupies him currently. My attention is divided; I can't help but wonder how much of what he understood from that *Tango* interaction had been accurately retold, I attempt to follow his current story of how wealthy people want experiences that can't be purchased or replicated, but that they precisely need to be replicated at the same time in order for people to keep having them, and all the while Sonny's voice is drowned and resuscitated by blender and ensuing silence.

"It's done!" he exclaims, as the chef hands him a bit of deep-blue goo on a small hand-hammered spoon. He takes the spoon into his mouth and pulls it out clean.

"Exactly!" he says. "Wow, yes! Now for the real test. Would you be so kind as to try?" he asks me.

"I'd be honored," I say. Never having been served food by a private chef, I am both eager to try and equally ashamedly aware that I am supposed to be a champion of equality.

But that is precisely why I'm here, and it would be rude to refuse, I mollify my psyche.

But instead of a spoon, the chef hands me something that looks like a mini paintbrush dipped in the goo.

I look to Sonny without a word.

"Brush it on your cheek," he says. "And be sure to note the exact sensation," he adds hastily.

"Brush it, oh, I don't, is it safe?"

"I just ate it," Sonny says in that same why-am-I-going-so-slow way.

"Like this?" I ask, stroking my cheek as though painting a fence.

Immediately the sensation of effervescence on my cheek of a lightness, of bubbles, of bubbles and bubbles, of buoyancy, not quite carbonation but a brightness, cool upon application followed swiftly by energy that isn't altogether warm, but vibrant and alive.

"What is this?"

"Describe what it feels like."

"It's cool, warm, light, almost weightless," I begin.

"No, what is it like? What does it remind you of?"

Without waiting for my answer, he takes another brush dipped in goo from the outstretched and waiting hand of his chef and lightly applies it to his forehead.

"Yes!!" he yells. "Yes, yes. This is it!" And after a second, "But it's still too brief. Three seconds, maybe less. See the problem?"

I look at the chef. His face gives away nothing but ambivalence.

"This is what it's like to be soda!" he exclaims definitively.

"Those are the words you were looking for," he adds. "Ever since that trip to Japan, I've thought, 'if only I could experience the things I love, I mean really experience them. Soda for example; I love soda, you see. And I thought, well why couldn't I experience what it's like to be soda, with my entire being.'"

He doesn't wait for my reaction. He doesn't need it. He speaks to me as if he's merely talking to himself and I, though in the room, just another corner of his mind with whom he can kick around his dilemma.

"I thought it was a sensuous type of pins-and-needles I was after. But *that* is only the result of *tasting* soda, you see. Soda itself wouldn't feel the sting of carbonation. It would be ebullient, the film of a bubble teetering on the action of, *pop*."

"But I want to feel this for longer. My idea is to be in a bathtub of it, much like soda waits for a consumer in a can. But this mixture dissolves within seconds of skin contact, or upon being consumed."

"If you create a shower to stand under," the chef speaks.

"One continuous stream," Sonny thinks out loud, finishing the chef's thought.

As subtly as possible I check my watch, but it isn't necessary for I have been completely forgotten, if I was even a thought to begin with. My thoughts drift once more over the pitch I had planned, explaining to Sonny what his money has been put toward this past year, the affordable housing that we managed to secure in the exact district he had himself recommended.

But as I listen to Sonny and his chef discuss the amounts necessary to have a five-minute experience, it feels pointless. So ridiculous is his problem, that bringing up the world outside his windows seems an unbroachable subject. Like a single member of a play suddenly pointing out how their house's 'back wall' is a two hundred seat theater. Obscene and unmentionable.

"Would you be amenable to testing once more? It doesn't work very well on hair and you are balding," Sonny says. I look at his coiffed black mane, combed back in thick streaks across his head into a wave of curls that crashes down the back of his head and onto his French collar.

He is attentive enough to see that he has hurt my pride. I'm unsure about having it poured over my head, and the sudden attention to my appearance, me as a *person*, brings me into the room so forcefully, it's as though I've just materialized here, naked.

"It's a blessing. This will be the most incredible experience of your life, I promise."

I know I can't say no. For Sonny, this is more valuable than all of the cars and dead-artist masterpieces, maybe even more prized than his seaweed experience in Japan. It has also dawned on me that Sonny has no idea why I have come, and to tell him at this point would be a humiliation for both of us. It would put a lasting taste into his mouth, a flavor vividly revisited each time the name of my charity was mentioned.

The chef hands the blender's carafe to Sonny, who stands quite a bit taller than me, I notice for the first time.

"It would be better to remove your shirt, just in case," he says, carafe already positioned above my head. My hesitation is too much for him to bear and he commences pouring the contents of the blender slowly and with the utmost care onto my *balding* head.

I become intangible. A soda, trillions of bubbles, no, the inside of those bubbles, more, I am the *fragility* of the bubble!, the thin layer of existence of ether air lightness, of a *pop*. I melt. I transform in an instant. As the goop pours over my head some cascades off of the not yet dissolved goop that has already made contact with my skin, enabling it to pour down my face. I close my eyes as it covers them gently, trickling over my nostrils and gracing my lips. In other rivulets, it channels off the sides of my eyebrows, over my temples and down the sides of my face, each millimeter figmenting me into nothingness. I cease to exist in the same moment I'm still there (I'm ceasing), a bubble mid-pop. I want to sing in rapture, in mind-altering elation. And then it's over.

I feel my face with my hands. The sensation of effervescent nothingness still coating me, though there's no proof left of the goo that covered my head only moments ago.

I look at Sonny, eyes wide. He knows what he has given me, even if I can't fully process it myself. There's nothing else for me to say. There's nothing else that he could give. Nothing for me to contribute.

During a short discussion with the chef, in which I continue to tingle with my nonexistence, my *popping* into intangibility, Sonny finalizes the quantities he wants the chef to work on creating so he can take a proper shower in it. He will shave his head bald for the occasion, he says with gleaming eyes.

The chef escorts me into the elevator and returns us to earth. On the way down he asks me if I tried the bed in the waiting room. I only shake my head, no. "No one does," he says. "He makes me ask everyone who comes just the same."

I meander out into the new midnight, the air thick with humidity. I feel my skin again but the sensation is gone, only the memory of what it felt like remains. Knowing Sonny is in good spirits, I should head to the office and send him an email from our company asking for his yearly donation plus extra. I won't mention the name Sonny or the fact that we met earlier this evening. I stumble through the night, disoriented. I repeatedly touch my face in different areas for signs of effervescence, to see if any areas *remember*, as though my touch might awaken the sensation. Though he has undeniably given me something of immeasurable value, I can't help feel like he owes me now because of it. Exposing me to that, an experience utterly erasing me as a human, I couldn't have been ready. I don't have the cars, or the paintings, or the private seaweed-harvesting experiences in Japan. I haven't built up to that level of existence, to the extent where I can spend my time conceiving of not being, or of being something other, like a soda.

CYLENDRICA

She's a rough maple-shaped wedge scything the town of Siem Reap's bucolic mural. The name *Calvin* buckshots the air; the sour disharmony of *Calvin* tears willow-chewing oxen from pastoral canvas. Young children in the shadows of rice fields fishing frogs look for the source of *Calvin,* and seeing her *crème de la linen* smear across the banana grove, infer her trajectory: the bungalow for tourists, and soothe a frazzled ox back into the calm state of a painting with coos of *ko ko.* Then they resume frogging.

Husband hums a luke-morning bath in salvaged citrus

"Mm, mm, mm, that loofah climber with the cylindrical fruit"

He's remembering someone who served them dinner perhaps, perhaps a sensuous fruit is just a sensuous fruit, perhaps it's nonsense, perhaps when he says, "let it bear that long angled luffa fruit," "Let it bear it," he's phantasming whispered spores.

I'm Luffa Cylendrica, green-washing alternative, your Egyptian Cucumber, Vietnamese Exfoliator, Cambodian Hot-Stone

"There's a trash heap out back! A huge fucking pile, Calvin!"

Husband, in a reverie of "tendrils," "coiling tendrils," hears the archangel, hears her on the phone with god above, Calvin of the Transcendent Journeys; how quickly does god answer the call of a beloved angel. Hark! He is already on a simultaneous call with the accommodation owner, Arun, asking about the trash pile only a short walk from the bungalow.

Third-person privilege into the secondary exchange:

C: a trash pile, my client saw a huge trash pile

A: out of sight, eighty meters away and on the other side of the banana grove

C: used bedding, plastic bags, plastic hangers, plastic toothbrushes, half-used bars of soap, tins of used cooking oil, what else, she said there was more

A: we don't have anywhere else to put our garbage, if someone takes it away it goes into a pile next to someone else's house

C: why all of the plastic, we were told you use renewables, bamboo toothbrushes and all that

A: we do, but we already had plastic hangers, and stock of plastic toothbrushes and tubes of soap, we can't afford to send it back, and to where

{Here, Arun stays on the line listening to Calvin sing his angel a lullaby on the other line, but she has just woken, she brandishes a trumpet, and she will sing a madrigal of guilt-free airfare, of a polyethylene-free forty-eight hours, and hot-water-used-for-dinner-used-for-baths-for-tea-for-watering-gardens}

Husband fingers citrus, skirts its floating cross-section across a film of botanicals, water cool and growing gelid, wandering Cylendrica flirting out of reach.

Communication severs, she inhales for a grand alleluia, an aria for her tub-wrinkled partner. It's a roundel,

"There's a trash heap out back! A huge fucking pile!" sails forth into a clear Cambodian sky, honey-coating the countryside in her Word.

БАБА

Baba: In any number of fairy tales I've been burdened with language not my own: *witch, jealous crone, forest spirit*, anything to do with being an *old woman*. I'm rooted in Eastern Europe but watch me metastasize as easily as a sneeze, dampening the pages of innumerable linguistic histories.

Though the mayfly suffers the worst of time's gravity, it manages to levitate. Or perhaps it is because of this transience that *time* becomes just another aspect of the mayfly's chaos. Contrariwise, I'm purling so slowly toward that inevitable chronology that I'm bloated with time for thinking about mayflies: how I could spend their entire lifetime poisoned on the floor of my cabin, or suffering a Catherine wheel, or staring up at a window, and call it a memory.

Of the names for the guillotine, of which there are many (e.g., *Louison, la demi-lune* (the half-moon), *le massicot* (the cutter), *la veuve* (the widow), *Mirabelle)*, my favorite remains *la monte-á-regret* (the regretful climb), this being the only moniker that takes into account the blade's feelings as its being raised.

And it was at its zenith that the blade, lost in thought, continued to deliberate its fate long after Monsieur de Paris had released the cord. *Something is wrong! The axe doesn't fall.* Anticipatory seconds contained the crowd's murmuring until, dam-sprung, a din of complaints enveloped those on the stage, briefly causing the players to forget their roles of arbiter, executioner, and official, the only exception being the condemned. From my vantage I saw only the movement of shadows above me, any of which could have been the blade descending. I wriggled my toes, aware once again that my footwear had been taken.

Long after the masquerade had ended—being very much unbeheaded—I was shuffled shoeless into a cell that had been left unlocked because of the fracas caused by the malfunctioning *bécane* ("the machine," as it was most commonly known). Upon returning to the woods I happened upon my shoes where *I* had taken them off earlier, beside a lush patch of moss that I had been working my toes between moments before my capture. Old age makes one careless and it's difficult to jump at the sound of every chirp or holler, as echoes have become an old woman's souvenirs, not to mention the burden of jumping.

I hadn't thought much on that stay of execution until somewhat later when some recondemnation or other had officials arguing over the ethics of firing squad vs. guillotine, myself being impartial to both. But apparently their contretemps stemmed from a medical experiment conducted by a certain Dr. Beaurieux, who had been granted permission to examine the head of a guillotined criminal/victim immediately upon execution. It had been observed that there was nothing unusual about the first few seconds of spasmodic contractions, but when the doctor called out "Languille," which was the name of the decapitated man . . . here one official broke from their discussion to read directly from Dr. Beaurieux's findings, so bizarre and inexplicable was the incident:

I saw the eyelids slowly lift up, without any spasmodic contractions—I insist advisedly on this peculiarity—but with an even movement, quite distinct and normal, such as happens in everyday life with people awakened or torn from their thoughts. Next Languille's eyes very definitely fixed themselves on mine and the pupils focused themselves. I was not, then, dealing with the sort of vague dull look without any expression that can be observed any day in dying people to whom one speaks: I was dealing with undeniably living eyes which were looking at me. After several seconds, the eyelids closed again[1].

Can the body feel the pain of severance without the mind to process pain? What *is* pain without the ability to process that sensation? Not inconsequentially, after it had been decided that the firing squad would be used, the gendarmes lined up and discharged. So overpowered was I by the *bang*, I would not have been surprised to know it was the sound alone that felled me. I felt something, certainly, but was unsure as to whether the bullets had found their mark.

In an attempt to spare the gunmen the certainty of having killed, it is often the case that one rifle in a line of gendarmes is unloaded. Over the course of various charges read against me, the details which are always obtuse, at no point has anyone said something akin to, *death by Monsieur de Paris, death by John Smith*. Never is it called by the name of *who* is doing the killing. The witch-hunt tribunals that had swept a fever across Europe

---

[1] Kershaw, Alister. *A History of the Guillotine*. (Taken from the *Archives d'Anthropologie Criminelle*, Dr. Beaurieux. 1905.)

employed the greatest linguistic escapism, since the burnings were *trials* and to survive meant one was guilty. All that claptrap to avoid cardinal sin, as they reasoned the firestarter wouldn't be committing murder since a witch won't burn and guilt was already assumed.

I met a man who repeatedly told me from across our makeshift holding cells that he wasn't a witch, but such conversations never require my participation. It wasn't until the day of his trial that he asked if there was any way to avoid being burned by the fire, as though my silence held some wisdom. I told him to admit to being a witch and then there would be no need for a trial.

"But they'll kill me."

"Yes, but they probably won't bother with the fire."

His last words were, "I know who I am." And then fire took him and he screamed. Villagers attempted the same thing with me three days later. The charges read against me, "You stand trial for being a witch." I explained their error, that they confused themselves. They said, "If you burn, you will be exonerated. If you don't, it confirms you are a witch." I said, "Maybe I'm a *rock*. Rocks don't burn. Maybe I'm a *myth*. Try burning one." They said, "You won't enchant us with such trickery." My conservation continues despite their language.

I have heard a story of a babushka whose own house was bedizened with hard candies, licorice, and sweetened breads to attract larger meals than birds. To go through such trouble for some company and a proper meal one must be quite lonely indeed, not necessarily mad though, just desperate enough to seem mad. If the only thing to eat was crow, I'd welcome anything that wasn't crow it should seem: though in the case of this certain babushka, why she didn't just eat the candies and bread might just mean she was mad.

Still it's sad, because some live in the woods removed from town somewhat, somewhat whispered about, and it's often the case that one babushka living in the woods begins sounding similar to another babushka living in the woods, especially when this is heard through whispers. But *Porgia will be home soon, and a meal eaten by two*: my delusional mantra.

Woods remain the same no matter where I reside in the world. And interestingly, woods are always familiar in the way that they shade, breathe, house more life than a city, and always have someone close by who fears them. Whilst living with Porgia, a woman's dying had distracted me from a note I had been composing.

Slumped against a tree and nearly immobilized from poison, she scanned the trees in frantic blinks as sweat drowned her vision.

"What have you done?" I asked, smelling the poison in her blood. She gasped but composed her fear well thereafter.

"I knew you'd come."

"And who am I?"

"The *bear*," she said.

"And you think I'll eat you?"

"That's why I took precautions and poisoned myself slightly."

"More than slightly," I responded. "You're dying. What did you use?"

"Snake," she smiled, showing me the two fang marks on her upper wrist.

I approached and took hold of her arm. Her hair held autumn light similar to how mine used to, and though she had heterochromia, her gold-speckled left eye matched the two of mine beautifully.

"Go ahead and eat me. You won't take anyone else from our village, demon," she said, ruining my moment.

"You are quite stupid," I explained. She lost consciousness while I bit into her arm, sucking out the poison to save the body from full contamination.

I returned to my cottage feeling quite ill, but composed a poem which I recited for Porgia.

> My pine needles shine
>
> with the sky's nimiety,
>
> the glut that morning's mist
>
> has hoarded onto these fir tips.

"Are you a tree?" Porgia didn't understand the poem and told me so.

"I'm not sure," I said. "I've been poisoned slightly, so it might not be any good."

I mention this story from my past as I am currently confined the floorboards of my cabin experiencing an acute nihility. In my periphery, thin gray strands of hair free themselves from the fibrous spindles of arachnidium (those cobwebs of neglect overrunning the cabin) and move upon the hearth where firelight spins its own gossamer over my vision and they are lost. My own geriatric trichobothria strain for a breeze;

---

[2] "*saudade é lembrança de alguma coisa com desejo dela*" —*Duarte Nunes de Leão*. I find this note stuck in the pins of a fat cactus that suffers from my over-nurturing, reminding me that its words have outlived my Portuguese. Have we met, Duarte? Do you have memories of me?

my thoughts churn in ennui! My sensilla cry, *saudade!*[2], which means nothing to those outside Portuguese. Or *Morriña*[3], specific to Spanish, Romanian *dor*[4]. Тоска[5] I forget. *Sehnsuch*[6] and *lebensmüde*[7] are just some remnants of me in German, like finding in one's attic broken sticks fastened to used silk having long since forgotten what a kite is.

I'm sensationalizing terribly I know, for I can hear my thoughts the loudest of anyone. But I won't stop: my brain the only part capable of travel in this moment. I *feel* for myself but exist only in thought. I have nothing to do but lose myself within these piles and piles of words, and I should note—which may help explain the glossolalia—that time has revealed its hidden clockwork to me and slowed, slowed, slowed everything down to this moment: stalled, whereupon I can witness the prestidigitation of time's empty gearbox, insight made only possible after being poisoned by witch's bane[8] for which the fault is mine

---

[3] Remainders of my past litter the cabin, oftentimes in languages I can no longer read. This note is illegible because of a deep red stain that had kept it fixed to the floor.

[4] I'm unsure if this relates to *dor*, but under my bed: "*Once when I was on the back hill of our garden in Mândra, a rainbow butterfly set on my right shoulder. A butterfly like I never saw and I will never ever see again.*" —*Alina Zara-Prunean*

[5] *Too many words not doing enough. Leave тоска alone*, found marking a place in a compendium of vegetables.

[6] I ate a child who had lived only a few years. Every choice is an infinity; even thoughts, which have even less existence than words. More Portuguese would have become me into something different. I think there is a deep, deep longing for something that likely doesn't exist.

[7] The word *translation* followed by a colon, followed by a word that looks like the German for *sigh*.

[8] I've heard so many names for the same thing: aconite, monkshood, wolf's bane, leopard's bane, mousebane, women's bane, devil's helmet,

for consuming a mouse I had found dead, even after swearing off meat since the last time I ate tainted human flesh. However long this mouse debilitates me, it won't compare to four days spent staring at the head of someone who looked enough like me to have the rare opportunity to see myself from outside myself: dead and on a floor.

I was once stoned (nearly) to death. I found out later that this was Porgia's fault, having had perhaps tried to spare me from myself (this incident was left unexplained like a lump in our relationship). Eventually, to confirm death, the stones were removed from the pit in which I was placed. They found me not dead and discussed stoning me once more on the chance that I had managed to survive due to some cracks or gaps in the rocks they had weighed upon me. I thought this must have been the case, too. I later asked Porgia what stoning should have felt like and Porgia described to me the sensation I felt upon finding out that Porgia was to blame.

There's a town near these woods that I haven't walked through in quite some time, precisely because I enjoyed the language of the central fountain, now lost; *burble* and *splash*. The last time I was there only two fish, a goldfish and a koi, remained of the original eight, which were all Prussian carp and their relatives. It's no longer novel but during the Jin Dynasty in China, when I had coveted a particular area of forest that contained a lone pine surrounded by a hectare of bamboo, I noticed a significant increase in the color variations of the standard silver carp,

queen of poisons, or blue rocket. I've pulled *witch* for this moment, feeling guilty and poisoned. Associations are inescapably ugly.

especially of the gold variegation, which people tended to cultivate in pools within their gardens and sectioned streams. This odd perversion was taken to the extreme when, later on, some Song empress forbade nonroyalty from breeding the golden variety. The memory of this unnatural selection has kept me from re-creating a lone pine in a forest of bamboo in some other part of the world.

To the reason I no longer visit the fountain: a monk that had fled his home in the Kuril Islands, troubled by the question of whether he resided in the Northern Territories as claimed by Japan, or the Southern Kurils as asserted by Russia. He found this fountain while soul-seeking and awaited the offspring of the goldfish and koi. The monk sat opposite me and sweat in neat little lines down his bald head while the goldfish hid in the shadow of the koi as the two toured the fountain, we four alone. After a period that shifted the sun's strength to the west, the sparsely carved column from which the fountain purged its water cast a long shadow that spared me from the rays. The monk continued to sweat and his seepage distracted me from the fountain so I readied myself to leave.

"You are quite old," he spoke at last. The statement was posited such that it could have been query or unequivocal fact.

"How old do I look?" I asked, amused.

"Two thousand," he said. There was no irony in his voice. I delved into how close he may have been to correct but I got lost somewhere in the Bohemian Forest, during which time the sun began its descent. Neither of us talked. The fish swam laps.

"I will never have children either," he said to me. "This koi and goldfish, they will have offspring. Did you know a koi and goldfish can mate? Only their offspring can't. In these two creatures I can see the end."

The fountain kept spitting water but the sounds that had arrested me ceased. The pleasant *burble* and *splash* had fled. This isn't hyperbole but a phenomenon known as *temporal anechoics*. It is similar to when silence results from a heightening of other senses but in this case it occurs not within the listener. Rather the silence emanates from the medium or vessel that has caused an emotional reaction within the listener.

The monk appeared to be aware of the fountain's transition into soundlessness because he spoke quieter when he asked one last question.

"Am I from the north or the south?" He looked into the silent pool as he spoke. I understood that the question was being asked of the fish but I was required to answer on their behalf.

"South," I said.

He got up and left. The sound didn't return to the fountain after his departure and I have ceased visiting.

Though I prefer silence to the clumsiness of speaking, knowing myself to be a groundskeeper ill-equipped at keeping so many of my tongues from falling into disrepair (Porgia often losing patience as I look for the word *bee* in some language or other, Porgia having already been stung by the time I communicate effectively), it's difficult to get beyond speech if I am to lance this swelling loneliness.

But sometimes I don't want to say, "Stribog brings oracles," though this is the case: of some "wind" or other bringing bad news. I suppose I should be thankful that I suffer many fewer winds than the Greeks, although I wouldn't mind a visit from the west wind, lovely even in Slavic. But this is not the point. I don't want to tell Porgia about Dogoda always missing our home or to have to calm a child with some anecdote about Eurus or Boreas looking Greek and uncomfortable so far from the islands, rapping at my windows when my sleep is in straits. I just want to say *babababababa* sometimes and be understood; or to not be alone and say *babababababa* or even nothing and just not be *mis*understood.

In Porgia's absence my voice becomes nothing but the endemic cackling of unseen crows or the wind looking for something. There was of course a time before Porgia, which my memory is in the process of contorting into an indeterminate period crammed with the lack of Porgia. Now when my mind cascades, so often are all the cataracts named Porgia and Porgia and Porgia and there was also that philosopher who kissed me before she was tortured and killed whose name will resurface when it pleases.

Just yesterday I followed a dewdrop down a vine until it rolled to the edge of a leaf: an ivy heart, where it hung in plump meniscus before falling to the ground. Years of being forested have endowed me with the gift to follow that water's dispersion into the soil where roots of a proximal bluebell plant extract the moisture from the soil. The plant matures; a cluster of tiny flowers like choir bells emerge and play their enchanting song to the delight of insects. A human life germinates in seed as well. A baby born, a baby born. We were all babies born. We can share in that. But though the forest reminds me that life is continual, which is hopeful, it's hard not to be offended when people don't recognize what is alive in me. But I think I have forgotten something about what is alive in me which could mean the same for others. Why am I so disconnected from being alive when I am alive? Isolation has made me crabby; I sometimes set fires in town. I torment the hunters walking the woods. I have eaten people and animals when it was easier than foraging. I pay dearly for these transgressions. Insomnia: the moon mimics the sun and my eyelids go missing.

It just so happened that the expansion of the Roman Empire coincided with a transitory period in my conservation where I thought I just might release myself from the forest canopy's omnipresent shade. And truthfully, while the expansion of the Empire could not have been entirely unrelated to my vagabonding, I distinctly recollect forswearing my relation to my two sisters after a falling-out that was fueled by our youth and an urgent need to unknot myself from the avoidable fate of becoming the stories that people told about us; this was already in the process of reducing me to an archetype of myself.

Shortly after a nameless conquest (so ubiquitous were they during this time that even the loss of eighty to one hundred lives was unremarkable), I found myself the unwilling participant of a hecatomb that wasn't living up to its name. The organizers had acquired ninety bulls for the sacrifice dedicated to the high Roman commander's battle prowess, but ninety wouldn't suffice and so it was left to lots that only two of the dozen cattle farmers would get to enjoy the festival.

For the chosen, it's difficult to see the difference between a sacrifice and an execution. I've noticed it spoils the mood of a sacrifice to have the offerings begging for their lives in the same way this strife heightens an execution. When the knife's plunge is one of sacrifice and not execution, is pain experienced differently? I had disguised myself amongst the bulls and so never found out, having had the foresight to weaken the paddock's back post with a swift kick while the organizers were forcing farmers to draw lots. No sooner had the sacrifice begun when the grounds were suddenly overrun by half of the bulls rampaging in no certain directions. And though the sudden transformation of spectators into unwilling participants painted horror across their faces, there had to be some yearning in that dread that spurred the people of Pamplona to voluntarily re-create this chaotic scene later in history.

During an especially pleasant incarceration locked in the rear of a wagon headed for Santiago de Compostela, my captors' superstitions kept me from ill-treatment as I was, at worst, a witch, likely just some woman, but possibly a saint. I was fed meat (being long before I swore off flesh), wine, and a story that I have tried to keep preserved in the Spanish it had been gifted to me, but time has suffered me a good deal of termite-like boring and none of my stories have escaped imperforated:

"A priest, having made the same pilgrimage by the Way of St. James to the holy site of Santiago de Compostela, came across a hermit in this exact forest. The hermit complained of seeing stars during the day and of the sun at night, so the priest, trying to understand this conflux, began asking questions: Do you see anything aside from these celestial bodies? Do you hear anything exceptional? Can you feel the warmth of the sun at night?

To all of these questions the hermit demurred. The priest, intrigued, asked if the hermit had found Christianity, to which the hermit was ignorant. The priest then asked to be permitted to spend a week's time with the hermit to show him the path of the Lord, to which the hermit was neither for nor opposed. So he unloaded his provisions and built a fire, startling the hermit as he had never seen fire and for the first time in his life felt a chill on the following day when its embers had died. Every night hence the hermit stayed close to that fire and recognized his own Thanatos as it waned. On the third day the priest broached a matter that had been troubling him greatly since encountering the hermit.

'How is it that you do not eat?' asked the priest.

'I eat from time to time: toadstools, dead flies from webs, water from moss, seeds yet to root.'

'But don't you get hungry?' asked the priest.

'What's *hungry*?' replied the hermit, and so the priest explained the concept of hunger to the hermit. He listened intently and then the two went to sleep.

Then next day the priest took his leave, giving the hermit a *pathetic* look that he himself would never understand the extent of, because not three days after his departure the hermit expired from the hunger the priest had given him."

The English word *pathetic* has shameful connotations and it's only through vigilance that I'm able to preserve it differently. Desiring connection, a *word* is created. It lives cautiously. It broadens and acquires implications; its outward appearance may change over time while its meaning becomes something else entirely.

Those scraps of paper that my hermitage often effectuates offer no recollection of from where they've alighted. Such will-o'-the-wisps might looks like this:

Middle French's pathétique: *moving or stirring*

Late Latin patheticus: *subject to feeling, sensitive, capable of emotion*

Greek pathetos: *endued with the capability to suffer, capable of feeling, liable to suffer*

1700's pathetic: *arousing pity, or pitiful*

1937 pathetic: *so miserable as to be ridiculous*

Despite illegibility and inevitable fading, I still occasionally make notes and set them free: to be found later or not. It's a way of talking without having to give voice to one's loneliness.

Of the many things carried by the wind is my name, a name carried so far and wide that it began to sound different depending on the place. I have yet to escape this name, it follows me across borders, reemerges when new empires are settled; it birthed me and I birthed it.

I had two sisters for a long period of my conservation. When *ѫжь* (wuž, the youngest) died and I wasn't there to bury her, अहि (*ahi*, the middle) called me *"jęza"* which at the time, *ahi* having taken to Old Church Slavonic, meant something along the lines of "disease." She whispered this word like a volley of arrows and these arrows struck other people. I was being translated into *iaga, inca, ekki, engti, jěžě,* and over the course of these disseminations my disfiguration became *Yaga.* Because of how long this moniker has persisted, it's often prefaced by *Baba* (old woman).

I am a declension of language, unable to shed the archaic hoard within me as fast as the non-me collective consigns it.

Something from my twenty-first-century imprisonment: Turkmenistan's President for All Eternity, much like the President for All Eternity before him, unveiled a huge golden statue of himself in commemoration of his reign to a diffusion of King Pigeons. We flew in the same direction and formed a beautiful wave that broke apart imperceptivity until I was once again swimming through the welkin alone.

It used to be that rock doves were used for such occasions. In one scenario *Arkadag*, one of President for All Eternity's self-fashioned names, would have spoken words of liberation from the previous dictator, of air to breathe in, of a fairer, *freer* Turkmenistan, at which cue-word the doves would have been released in such a flutter that people would've cried in wonder that the sound of their heart's excitement could be so faithfully reproduced. And hours later when the people had returned to their homes, so would the homing doves have circled back to their cages.

President for All Eternities (made plural as a precaution and to demonstrate his foresight), brilliant as he was, had known this and certainly wouldn't have wanted to risk comparisons in the form of words or whispers, or photographs captioned with such lines as *falsely freed*, so he used all-white King Pigeons that were truly free when released. Quite visibly, his magnanimity had brought tears to his eyes.

But he had miscalculated; he hadn't counted on people finding them in the streets, torn apart by predatory birds, killed by cats, and starving for lack of any necessary skills. Domestication has left them this way. I knew this about them and still chose this brand of liberty, seeing little difference as it is between freedom and captivity. When one is a bird and can become more, by which I mean taking flight amongst a skein of beings sharing a consciousness, it's worth incarceration, it's worth the fragility of hollow bones and the constant tears of mid-flight and . . . this is what humanity has forgotten, to be moving together. The importance of a moment like this one will be lost to the inadequacy of words; it is as beautiful as the sunrise would be if I knew it to be the last one.

I will struggled with how to present my language. The truth of my verbage is-was-will be a deformation of the future to past, present to future, past to present-future.

I will been, I have being, I currently was.

My conservation was be a stasis of catching up with what will passed; the grammatical vice and rack at work now was the pure state of my language: tortured. Describing my language can't touched the process. Only from using what will had been wrestled from me pre-speech and henceforth sacrificed it to the air could the abomination of my strife be hearing accurately. It was maddening, echoes will propagated in thoughts I haven't yet think. Nights of isolation have challenge me to look beyond a star's timid twinkling for what will already exploded. Eons-past starlight will touches my process.

There was a slice of history's leavening loaf whence I was waiting for a bus in *Bălgrad*, a town of such scarce populace that encountering another waiting in tempo for the same bus, and a sobbing man at that, was a rarity that likely never re-capitulated. He bawled *pathetically*, and being that there was no one else, I interposed. It had been quite some time since I had included myself amongst someone else's future memories, which is certainly why I remember this exchange for it broke my long fast of human interaction. Without hesitation but still thick with blubbering and speaking a Romanian I remember quite clearly (which reminds me we could have not been waiting for a bus but likely had been fetching water on the Mureş River), this man explained that he had secretly been in favor of some minor rebellion that had just been quelled, the three leaders captured. But it cruelly fell to him to administer Joseph II's justice, decreed as "breaking on the wheel." What alliance of fate had caused me to dine on my own past in that moment, and who now strokes my mortal coil so to induce such a waterfall of recollection?

"This punishment is not uncommon, far cry," said Erdel (we never exchanged names). "Only I have never seen its implementation." This followed a bout during which Erdel was incapable of speech. "I fastened Horea to the wheel. There was a crowd. I wielded a club." He was readying himself to cry again, at which point I interrupted.

"You have it all wrong," I said.

"Pardon?"

"He isn't to be fastened to the wheel. He is to be bludgeoned *with* the wheel."

"I, I-I, can that be right? It was decreed, 'breaking *on* the wheel.'"

"What century is this?" I asked.

"I'm—I'm not sure I understand the inquiry?"

I contemplated the differences in our Romanian. He had yet to point out the antiquated errs on my part (which he did in fact do at some point that will not be mentioned).

"What is the year of our lord?"

"Seventeen-eighty-five," came from Erdel with unnecessary speculation as to my well-being.

Of course, so the year was 1785, which I could not

remember until I asked him. In all likelihood I never asked him and have just retroactively asked him this to confirm from where I pull this memory, as 1785 might mean something more to someone else.

"Eras ago," I began explaining to Erdel, "we—rather, it was called a Catherine wheel. It was adorned with spikes. Do you know who Saint Catherine of Alexandria was?"

"I'm sorry, I don't," Erdel said, sounding sincerely apologetic.

"When the inquisitors attempted to lash Catherine to the wheel it broke upon her touch. Wait. I may have confused her with Hypatia. Either way they were both murdered. What I intended to talk about is that I saw it used properly in Gaul."

"Where's Gaul?"

"Oi, that is to say France. The condemned was lashed and lain upon a portion of road where natural grooves formed and a drawn wagon was then pulled over me—eh, the condemned. This process would be repeated as necessary, and one could survive for days. Though I imagine your method finalized quickly?"

"Yes, well," Erdel said growing quiet.

I don't remember fetching the water, which is why it first struck me that I had been waiting for a bus, but I do remember Erdel quite well. At this point, the earth has finished decomposing his body. I try not to let the same thing happen to his words within me, as I must be their sole harbor, though they float in the quagmire of my confluent linguistic goulash.

When I touch my arm I hear not the moment of bone cracking under the wheel, but Gallic voices in concert with one another inflicting their language upon me for the first time.

I see the young girl, a stranger to me, whose pupils had become engorged with something like hate—from where had she pulled this? My eyes met those of a young boy whose sympathy betrayed him as someone who would suffer greatly in this world, who, it was plain to see, felt so much more than I was feeling that it risked defining him. For such people like him to have existed gives me hope, though I wished in that moment to have numbed my thoughts by staring into the tranquil eyes of someone who would never understand.

I stop here to give voice to Hypatia who kissed my lips while we both were bound (centuries before *Bălgrad*), though I knew her well before our proximate torturing. In a dissimulation of birds I had arrived on a southwest wind that hardly penetrated the air's violent mephitis. From a rooftop with other birds, I listened to her lecture in beautiful Greek on mathematics and astronomy. Even as an unabashed pagan in a land burgeoning with religious hostility, her composure and self-assuredness had me believing myself to be her younger, which naturally couldn't have been the case although I was quite young retrospectively. With her, one felt a sense of home that comes not from any location, thus I had no reservations about offering myself as myself, she having impressed upon me the fatally vanguard qualities of hope and progressiveness, notions about which (unfortunately for me) haven't changed much since that Bohemian stint. How is it that humans are still using the word *progressive* for the very same fish that were gasping during my youth? Language doesn't know how to crucify those in control of it; bah, I'll stop avoiding the end.

Her death has become me greatly, both of us having been denuded and flayed ὀστράκοις, meaning oyster shells. She remained conscious as her skin was peeled with ceramic tiles, though this was attempted shortly after on me with oyster shells because Hypatia's skin had impossibly broken every tile, and throughout she had offered nothing save a whisper, loud enough to be intended only for me, "I can still love humanity."

(   ) echoes (that) free themselves from the sound of water collecting in a disused well take turns distorting themselves in spectral elegy as they climb the damp stones toward freedom— next to which I am slumped from caducity. My ears glom on to a baritone singing, *gorbia, gorbia,* and a quavering alto chorus of *poi poi poi.* How voice-like the sound, how nonliving.

Sorrow's fatigue has webbed my ears; I'm sure I've heard the melody incorrectly. I survive Porgia (I envy the).

The following poem is titled: *A bad love poem for Porgia.* It's never been given sound.

My first warm snow was a Siberian equinox,
no fern no frond: small contorted flakes.
Hurriedly shamefully commuting. Avoiding
the skin, the trees, the ground,
evaporating in the instance of another's gravity.

Porgia may have thought in me, "There is no love for Porgia within a vessel so deep with time." *Oh, Porgia,* there is no love like one's current love; everything current is infinite: e.g., an open cut.

Desiring connection, it was either myself or Porgia who suggested living in town (I remember quite well who it was). Living in a line of interconnected buildings near the central market, Porgia opened our south-facing window and asked me if I felt the pulse of life; just then a silent eulogy for my pulsing loss, so much less life in town than forest. I assuaged Porgia's doubt by lying, retreated to the forest daily, brought plants to live in our house and deposited more in a box out front, and out of guilt transplanted them back to the forest the following day.

Back to town one afternoon with only thoughts of the glade I had napped in to find our house on fire. Porgia didn't jump from the window or even open it. I saw those eyes through spectral glass in need of cleaning, trained on mine, their turquoise drained. Why didn't Porgia call out, why was it me? *This is pain*, a rupture not from any one place—as if our souls could be in any one place—steeping within me, followed by the dilution of time that lulls one into thinking the pain has left. Boughs of dried rosemary and garments with grass stains can still draw grief.

A small collective came to put out the fire, rather: to keep it from spreading. Neighbors left their homes with belongings in fear of contagion. In the end, a home-size gap was left between two untouched houses. I stayed in the forest that night and returned the next morning to sift for Porgia in the cold shadows of the looming homes to the melody of a piano permeating a wall, which sounded something like being forgotten.

Ubasute (A custom in which elderly or sick members of society are taken to remote locations to die): it must have been that I met the monk from Kuril long after I had lived in Sloping Forest on the edge of the Chiers River. That was in Titelberg, pre-Roman consumption. What are they calling it now? Anyway, I remember the place as one of my few fond memories, as natural springs bubbled up and made bathing pleasant year round. The people of the region referred to me as *Sirona*, obviously confusing me for a deity. They spoke Celtic; no, it must have been Celtiberian. Before I was able to converse with them they would cry this name into the woods and leave a sick woman or child behind for me to care for. My sisters were still alive at this point and it was because of them that I was eventually driven out of the oppidum. Come to think of it, that may have been the last time the three of us were together, one of them having killed and eaten a child in my care. One gets tired of hiding.

What I wanted to mention is that the aforementioned phenomenon of the fountain's *temporal anechoics* compelled me to search out the monk's Kurilian homelands. The displeasure of crossing the taiga and then a sea of relentless wind with a scarce amount of food was exacerbated by the barrenness of the islands the monk called home. The first two I visited had no human inhabitants and a nonexistent canopy. The largest, however, had a forest and sulfuric hot springs, which is perhaps why I brought up my conservation in Titelberg. It happened that when I was bathing and especially thoughtless an old woman startled me, quiet as a deer; it was the feeling of eyes on me that broke my mindless trance. I hadn't been in Kuril long enough to speak with this woman though she didn't attempt to engage me. She continued on deeper into the forest without a basket or satchel for collecting food and she was underdressed to disadvantage. I followed her with a crow to a grove that smelled strongly of cedar and it was here that she slumped against a tree and closed her eyes. I *cawed* to let her know I was present.

"Old crow, leave an *older* woman to die. I am exhausted and a burden to my family. This is my final contribution," she said not in the language of the island. She cried briefly but was too tired to continue. I kept other animals in the area away until she had died. There was no final indication, no defiant exit, no silencing of screams when immolation had become too intense, no noose, no limbs severed, no head rolling and no crowds of people to watch. But it was still impossible to view her departure as peaceful because the loneliness that saturated the air whispered of a death not without anguish.

But it was more than how *she* died; I was aware of the hollow that had slept into *me*, that which had happened each time a life (that had experienced me) quieted. Just as I keep Porgia alive with remembrance so too must I have been kept alive by Porgia. How many times must one endure tiny deaths until, at last, there is nothing left?

I am reminded of a place I've never been:
Aokigahara, a sea o' trees devoid o' birdsongs and cicadas' incessant mourning,
space
thick with something like air, that one breathes but never exhales.

NEVAR

I started spelling my name backward. I didn't think mom would mind like Miss Deshwain minded. A *smart nine-year-old girl like* me *doesn't need to cause trouble* {my age being used *as a behavior modification technique*}. And I didn't think Miss Deshwain would need to have a *parent-teacher* for *something so silly* {mom agreed}. Mom is great mostly and I think she only minded because Miss Deshwain minded. Because when Miss Deshwain minded something about one of my classmates, their parents had to come in for a meeting to be minded and reminded until the meeting was over and everyone was sorry they'd had to sit through that. And you could always tell when a classmate had suffered a *parent-teacher* because the next day they were all quiet and wouldn't make eye contact with Miss Deshwain. The worst was when Martin's *share-time* was inauspiciously scheduled for the day after one of his many *parent-teachers* and Miss Deshwain ended up explaining his baseball card {all wrong I found out during recess} because Martin didn't want to talk. He just held the card up in his hand for us all to see and looked at the floor for three minutes and forty-three seconds {Sammy said she counted} while Miss Deshwain *botched it.*

But I'm not like Martin or even Sammy {Sammy is a girl and sometimes my friend, though that's not important}. I behave in school, I really do. There is not a *rebellious bone in this body*, except maybe the ones that caused me to run into the street when I was only four that nearly got me *flattened like a pancake* by a car, causing mom to shout some indelicate words she assured me later she had never said. And even those accidentally rebellious bones didn't mean it; it was more of a stumble as I wasn't used to running yet and my muscles were, are, still developing; and the doctor said they will still be developing through my teenage years. *Growth spurts and growing pains and that's not all* {the doctor winking to my mom like she was *in on something*, but she wasn't tolerating anyone *talking about me like they knew me*, especially on her *one and only day off a week*}.

Then there's the dentist that we only go to sometimes because he's expensive, because in America we don't have dental care. *Maybe in Europe you can get all the cavities you want, but here you need to look after those pearly whites.*

We were allowed to write poems in Miss Kerlain's English class and I wrote about my teeth {she wasn't sure what to make of it, asked if mom helped, then because it's supposed to have comments from her, she scribbled, *I think the lines should be shorter, like poetry*}.

Baby-tooth aches, the sinister pleasance of twisting tooth from gums, tongue jumps across the gaps, tests the gaps, falls in love with the gaps, new construction, Venice houses leaning every-which-way, appraisals for architectural beautification, mom not having any of it, barely enough room to floss so give it up, Japanese shoulder to shoulder commuters on a train, wisdom teeth somewhere in the back trying to get off, the bustle up front, so much business near the doors when we need to get our smartest teeth out into society, appraisals for professional commuter removal *when the other commuter's don't comply, mom not having any of it, all the while flossing sporadically the wilted greens mom still cooks even though she's grandma's age by now.*

Miss Deshwain is right, I really can get a good tangent going and forget all about the class activity like that time we were supposed to be sinking rocks in water to learn about density but I already knew what was going to happen with that pumice stone and suggested tying it to a string and attaching some igneous rock with that pretty gneissic banding, but she wasn't interested {Miss Deshwain is my science *and* homeroom teacher, *a double whammy*}. I just thought we could have some density competitions and maybe bet on the stones like they do in horse racing {the cross-country kind}. I don't even have anything but my lunch to bet {and nobody, not even me, wants their dessert to be fruit and vegetables, especially when I know there are cookies in the house that mom hides for after bedtime}. I'd recently read about some guys who *looked into* that *Hidalgo* story, which was made into the Disney movie that I picked out of the bargain bin because of the horses.

Well, get this {that's how mom talks to her friend Jemma}, it's about a {fictional} horse race in the Middle East called the Ocean of Fire which was {*under no circumstances*} based on a true story. I watched it once before I snooped around on the internet, and then I watched it after my snooping and I still didn't care about it being {*under no circumstances*} *based on a true story*. I still want to race painted horses across a desert and have everyone rooting for me. And somehow that *desire ended up manifesting* in a rock-density competition played out in plastic food containers that I noticed said *Rubbermaid*; and I couldn't understand for quite some time why the ones at my house said *Rubbermade* until I looked it up online and discovered that ours were the generic, *cheaper* brand, like *Fruity-Os* or *Honey Nut Crispy Oats*. And one last thing before I stop doing what Miss Deshwain is always complaining about, {*tangents*} {and I really like this {} shape instead of parentheses but I don't know what they are called or if they are appropriate but *kids should be allowed to explore the computer world so long as it's nothing nefarious*}, why did cereal companies copy the popular brands? Mom said *we don't need brands that can't be original and we certainly don't need sugary cereal first thing in the morning.* And I've been meaning to ask her if that applies to *Rubbermade,* though I found out we had *Rubbermade* after the supermarket cereal incident {when mom explained about *cereal knockoffs* and sugar {and cavities as well} at warp speed because we were *double-parked* because of the snowstorm}. And she really had to *talk me down* from wanting that cereal too, even though it was only honeyed *Crispy Oats*. We laughed about it later. *It's not creative at all,* to steal someone else's cereal ideas like that. We laughed at the name the most; there isn't a kid in my class who would want to eat *Crispy Oats,* even if they taste the same as the one that cartoon honeybee is *peddling.*

But it's sad. I feel bad for the sham-cereal. It's just copying a popular cereal, so already it won't be as popular, and then you give it a name like *Crispy Oats,* how can it ever be popular or make friends. Oh, I think *a psychologist would have a field day* or even *a field week* over that last sentence and what it might say about me and my spelling my name backward on my work assignments. I shouldn't blame my insecurities on mom for giving me a name I wanted to turn backward. She's doing a great job all by herself.

But {and this is a big conjunction}, I was also thinking that my name {when spelled as mom intended} might be *culturally telling* and I worry that when it's time to get a job I will be *profiled* even though profiling is bad and people are really *cracking down on it*. I hope mom is right about *us getting our time in the sun*. She usually follows up her wistfulness swiftly with something uplifting, but occasionally she forgets and says, *a girl* my *age shouldn't worry about such grown-up things*.

Sometimes I pretend mom is the villain of my life-movie, that she says things like *don't worry about grown-up things,* because she's going to make sure I don't make it to adulthood, despite all of the vegetables and no cookies {just to trick me}. I know that psychologically I created this game to keep me from thinking too hard about impossible things, like why someone who has never met me might be mean to me. But still, I like to plan how I will record our conversations {once I have a cell phone, but I have to save my allowance because *cell phones don't grow on trees* even though I explained it would take seventeen years at *the current going rate* and I'd probably have a career by then to buy my own cell phone, to which mom said *great, you can buy me a new one too*} for evidence against mom who is planning to make sure I don't become a full grown-up {just grown-up enough to buy her a new cell phone and then *it's the axe for me!*}. It's a fun game and sometimes I look for clues by analyzing her speech patterns.

I'm only joking around, *I swear* {swearing in the sense that *I swear* is a heterological phrase, not actually swearing with words *we don't use in our house*}, but it would be a real fun competition to be challenged by mom, if she was planning an *elaborate and deadly game,* and I had to be smart enough to figure out the hints and rules to survive. I read about lions throwing their cubs off cliffs to toughen them up, but then I read that that's just a misconception that was started in a fourteenth-century Japanese epic. *What does Japan know about lions?* mom asked when I gave her *the headlines* {because sometimes mom likes *the headlines* instead of the whole story because *I have been known to recite an entire book, and that's no lie either, Jemma,* she told Jemma while Jemma did her hair. But apparently enough people are talking about lions tossing cubs if I'm still reading about it during the age of internet and special effects {when will the effects no longer be special?}. *Oops, tangents* {Sorry, Miss Deshwain}.

Senora Silva is our Spanish teacher but she's from Brazil. She speaks Spanish {sometimes} but I'm not convinced our school did a very good job vetting her for the job. I first had the idea to start writing my name backward in her class {and quite unintentionally, I promised mom after I told her about this: *that when you write it normally and then backward, black becomes white.* But I didn't mean it as desire to escape my skin color, at least not intentionally}. Senora Silva didn't seem to mind. But she spends a lot of the class time not minding. When it's *trabajo de clase* time, she checks her cell phone behind her desk. And Martin {who was told to use *Martín* as his *Spanish name* in class, but only responds unless Senora Silva refers to him by the appellation, *Pedro,* to which Martin follows-up by adding, *the best baseball player of all time,* a phrase that he sidekicks with getting out of his chair to swing an imaginary bat that always gets a response from Senora Silva to *siéntate,* and sometimes when she's really flustered, *sente-se!*} uses that time to copy off of Maria's worksheet. He used to copy off of mine, but since I knew he copied me I wrote down wrong answers and changed them later. And he still hasn't figured out why my sheets get little piñata stickers and his got red ink. He says that he doesn't even want *stupid piñata horses,* but they aren't horses, they are unicorn piña-ta stickers and sometimes abominable snowmen and Bigfoot and Nessie piñata stickers. And also, that's *psychology one-oh-one,* pretending he doesn't want cryptozoology piñata stickers when everyone gets so excited for them that we don't even mind that Senora Silva is likely teaching us a mixture of Portuguese and Spanish {which I know for sure is true because Maria's name is actually Maria and she speaks Spanish at home but still has to take the class because *everyone has to take the class,* and *pay attention* and *do the activities even if you already you know the answers, or the outcomes to certain science experiments, or English vocabulary, or math riddles*}. So that's why I got a *parent-teacher* for Miss Deshwain's science lesson, because I was bored and suggested a pumice versus orthogneiss duel and wrote my name backward. *I have to take it easy on Miss Deshwain* because I don't think Miss Deshwain has time to understand me, not completely, not with *thirty-five other little misfits to keep an eye on because the science equipment is old enough as it is and the school can't afford new equipment unless the parents want to donate or get out there on the streets and change people's minds, especially the older folks, and not just help out for an hour or two when people are driving to the schools to vote* yes or no *on the school's budget, because that's your daughter's future wrapped up in that word,* no.

One look from mom and Miss Deshwain stopped her complaining. I think it's because mom is a social worker and has *a good rapport with people,* even strangers. Or maybe it was grown-up code, but Miss Deshwain sighed. Mom reached forward and held her hands. I wanted to add mine to the pile but knew better than that. On the walk home {we live close to school}, I asked mom what it meant when she touched Miss Deshwain, just to be sure I knew. She said, *girls like us have to stay one step ahead and look out for each other because we are starting out so many steps behind.*

I nodded knowingly and mom laughed.

"I know a lot," I insisted.

She was quiet for a moment while we walked, and I knew she was contemplating what to say next because of her nonvisual eye movements.

"Raven, when you hug me, what does it mean?"

"It means, *I love you, mom*," I told her matter-of-factly.

"Do you think that every time you hug me?"

"Yes," I said, even though it wasn't true. But I didn't want to hurt mom's feelings.

"How about when you hug me suddenly when you are scared?"

"Well, when I'm scared," I thought for a second, "I'm just scared, but I still love you then, too," I said.

"So, it doesn't have to mean something specific."

"No, I guess not," I conceded.

"Sometimes we connect with people without thinking or knowing, and it has a meaning we can feel but can't explain."

Then she gave me a big hug and I couldn't help but thinking, *I love you, mom*, because we were just talking about it. But even when I'm not thinking it, I love mom, and she loves me even more; I just know it even though I don't know how.

PAOLO AND NIC. OR

SANDCASTLE AND CAVE-COLLAPSE

Crystal growing kit in hand, Paolo starts on the seal under a hand-crank flashlight, *I'd rather make this with my dad,* again he says. *I'll buy you a new kit when we escape.* I don't say *We are suffocating from the darkness alone.* Life rots into life, geothermal vents, warmth, sulfur, blind tetras, star-mimicking glowworm larva, water, *don't drink the water.* Handcrank light lullabies: gear-catch to shadow our cave for sparse intervals. Thirteen of us; huddled around our depleting oxygen, nascent crystallizations growing into spires, twinkling in the toxic pools and glowworm sludge. Slumbering on me like piglets, a litter of temporary sons, shaggy heads ebb on my rise and fall, shallower heartbeats until, for a fistful of beats, I drift back into an apartment that I loved with someone covered in vines and books. Sunset blur. Waking in a cave. How can we leave so easily, a hole blasted open, delirious as I am for our durance to become air and evaporate, how is it I validate my life, creating this temporary

Grabbing fistfuls of beach-sand to ooze between her tiny digits, my sister asks if, she wonders, if we can live here. We can build moats around moats around a castle within eyesight of mom who'll supervise with sparse encouragement from her sunglasses from her chair and the maw of a summer book my sister yanks her from every time she runs over for a drink. Let's work on the walls, and then the towers, but they are mainly heaps of sand and drip-drip spires. I dig a trench around a widening ellipsis of protection that reaches my knees. My sister will be swallowed within the walls, legs too little unable to hop that two-legged jump when the moat deepens. She'll dig a hole for the seaweed and broken-reed peoples she preserves. We'll sit within a ring of moats as the tide comes in, wrecking walls, surrounding us completely as I wonder against all inevitability if the castle will last; my sister just as enreveled to see us get swallowed by a rising tide, yelling *in-dependence!,* to the seaweed. I'll see my *family*, how do I continue unspooling a tethering to this blackhole, a single moment, how the kids didn't feel any time passing, or see that they had a father in me before we were all pulled, fighting an urge to say the crystals hadn't finished castle anew, that it's her prison, and my mom elsewhere, who doesn't notice the walls crumbling, that I need help, that it's *melting into the ocean*, my sisters' words stomping through the waters that stop rising within reach of my mom's towel.

LEM 'N' ME

"*I stole an ice cream truck,*" I yelled to Lem. She stood in line for a free piece of cheese at Calorie-Mart wearing her only sweatshirt like it was too heavy; though that white tag sticking out at the neck was screaming, *small!* Lem couldn't hear from way down in it, dragging herself shuffle-stop through that line like she had landed but couldn't shake the parachute. Bad simile.

"*I marched up and said, You all tangled up again?*" I meant that chute she was wearing. All she had to say was something like, *yeah* to let me know that I was there with her, but she was busy grousing at the already snaky line even though Calorie-Mart hadn't been open for hardly an hour; yep, and I thought from the way she swayed that she hadn't eaten or maybe there was some of that tinnitus caulking her ears because she didn't even have a one-liner holstered when one snake-liner had started hissing about some of the *people* in line, like "*people*" and "people" were two different things, like Lem wasn't already the most *person* it was possible to be without going crazy; so I answered my question for her, "*Yeah.*"

"*You gonna make it, Lem?*" But what I was thinking was, "I'm here, Lem!" I felt I was barely something when she was like this so I pulled out a memory as atonement for something I had done but couldn't understand.

"Here's a food memory to munch on." I just wanted to tide

her over through the ten-people-back torture she must have been feeling in that line. She wasn't usually so far I couldn't hand her a simple memory but it fell between us, or she got it and dropped it or didn't remember it so I reminded her.

"It's a croissant memory. Eat it! The one we got from Au Bon Calories."

Lem wouldn't look, her strawberry hair thinner in the halogen light. She just wanted the cheese, cheese made for rats getting digested in snaky lines. But *"I have an ice cream truck outside! I yelled again."* My hands twitched the way they do but my brain finally stopped scratching. The rats in line were staring only at me. Others shuffled their overfilled carts cautiously by like they already owned the stuff. Two clerks shot me full of disagreeable eyes but I deflected 'em right back.

"Come on, Tag, let's go," I said to myself, pretending Lem's voice.

"What do you want, Tag? I'm doing this for us but you're gonna get us kicked out again," Lem said so strained that it came out hushed.

"I knew you'd be cheesing today. Phantom Food posted it on their door this morning, I said. Phantom Food is a homeless shelter notice board that posts all the goodies and where to find 'em."

"Stop doing that," Lem said.

"Doing what?"

"You're narrating again, saying, 'I said' out loud when you talk. And I don't want people to know I'm looking for a handout," whispering *handout* even quieter than usual.

"Why'd you come to Calorie-Mart on free cheese Saturday then?"

"It's not free cheese Saturday," she whispered. *"It's just Saturday. These are samples. You know that, so stop fooling."*

More whispering. Wind tunnels were the worst. Lem lived in wind tunnels and made herself distant.

"Lookout, I'll give you a hand," I tried to whisper. The line was still Friday-evening-long but Lem stayed in line, eyes down; she got awful thin with me sometimes. I'd make up for it. I weaved between those people like they were nothing but traffic cones. Bad simile.

"And guess what? I yelled! They're nothing but traffic cones!" I was looking behind me but walking forward. Lem had quite a look: puzzled and jigsaws I was having trouble piecing, somewhere between fright and attentiveness and I crashed into a pyramid of soda-*zero* which created a mess of cans and people all around me. The line evaporated and the lady handing outs of cheese tried nudging her makeshift stand further from my orbit.

"I was yelling, No calories, No calories!" and rubbing rolling-cans all over my body. Lem was grabbing cheese, apologizing to the lady, *"He's got an illness,"* stressing *illness*.

I found Lem outside taking stock of her hoard, a mother bird about to eat all her little baby birds. Chick, chick, cheese.

"Before you eat those cheese-birds," I began. *"But I stopped talking because a cop was writing out a parking ticket on my ice cream truck."*

"So you really did steal an ice cream truck?" Lem said from impossible distance, faraway small. I thought to Lem, "Why do you keep littling yourself," but didn't ask because I was already saying, *"I should not have parked here, officer. Fine me to the max!"*

"This your truck?" he asked me like I'd done some magic trick he couldn't work out. Bad simile.

"No, sir," Lem said. *"I feel sorry for whomever it belongs to though,"* she said, scolding those blues of hers at me, but the shame she was hoping for got lost in the transit of her giving

me those two eyes for a few seconds. He finished writing the ticket and stuck it in the wiper. A seventy-five-dollar ticket. I didn't want to waste calories on a laugh, but seventy-five dollars! Oh, "*Seventy-five dollars! Seventy-five dollars, Lem!*" I thought and yelled the same thing. The cop sauntered off. I'd put that ticket on the fridge I didn't have with the food that wasn't in there when I needed a laugh I shouldn't want to have because laughter burns all those calories up.

"*Let's case those cheese cubes in wormwood and poison our ears with rotisserie wheels! Then we'll feast on ice cream, I said.*"

Lem ignored my toast and inhaled some cheese. She was tired and I knew I shouldn't be saying all that stuff about poison and ice cream trucks and soda cans because it turned her see-through.

"*Do you remember how to drive?*" I asked her. "*She munched away. She offered me a piece and I gobbled it.*"

"*Do you even know how to drive?*" she asked, knowing full well I didn't.

"*That's why my wheels are up on the 'walk, but now I have you here.*"

"*To be your accomplice?*"

I looked at her hopefully. We'd been through more together than her weak glare let on. We waited until the officer left, until Calorie-Mart had a rare gap between people shuffling in empty, shuffling out full, giving Lem time to lecture me about returning the truck.

"*If you drive, I'll take us back to my crime scene.*"

I gave precise directions and Lem negotiated the big ant maze as if she had never left the thorax of society. At a red light she sank into something that looked like deep vacancy, but became suddenly alert again when she received green. I stared in amazement at the acute transition until she felt me.

"*Some things you never forget, huh?*" she shrugged, voice brushed with melancholy.

After three more turns and a long narrow drive Lem dawned with recognition; I noticed from her perceptible forward lean. She took frequent holidays from her dashboard view to confirm her eyes against mine where we were going. She crept so slowly I heard the ice cream freezer churning louder than the dirty engine.

"*Just a little farther,*" I said, but she knew where we were.

"*This isn't where you stole the truck, is it,*" Lem said.

Suddenly nervous, suddenly thinking Lem might not have liked my surprise, suddenly terrified that Lem would leave me; so suddenly to be alone.

"*How did you remember how to get here?*" she asked, tears in her eyes. "*It's been a year since we've been to the wharf. A year exactly.*" Her voice drifted off. I couldn't weigh her emotions; which were heavier, which sank, which floated, which commingled. So often I needed her to tell me, but a sudden lonely fear kept me from asking. I didn't want to tip something over.

We sat in this limbo, staring out at the water clean enough to wash clothes, too dirty to drink. Cement pillars supported bridges that vehicles danced over and under. The sky clouded and the sun broke through to stare at the water too, but beat a retreat when it caught me looking up at it.

Lem got out of the car and moved toward the bay. I grabbed ice cream from the back and followed at a distance that, I had learned, gave her thoughts room to stretch. She walked so slowly across the gravel she was soundless. I followed behind less so.

"*You're too skinny, Tag,*" she said, not looking at me. Water crested against the edge of the embankment but still only managed to reach a couple feet below where we stood. We looked down at the water for some reason and I knew the silence was at work like the water was at work even though I didn't know what it was doing other than being there.

"*I don't want to be here,*" Lem said.

"*I gave her a look to say, are you sure?*"

"*I'm sure.*" Lem said.

The silence was a sailboat stalling. I waited for something, for some wind-kick, paper-cup-teeter, wrapper-shiver, for Lem's breath to say, "Well, okay, moving on," "Well, no, staying here."

No signs though.

How quietly did I say, "*This is where your son lives. I'm going to give him ice cream.*"

Her exhale wasn't quite a sigh.

I unwrapped a handful of orange creamsicles looking like dynamite and hucked 'em into the bay. They spread apart in the air and splashed with the sound of things that wouldn't sink; Lem flinched. I was remembering the jar of Sam we let float out on the water, how Lem was looking like she regretted letting it go. Lem was probably remembering the same thing even without me giving her a memory.

But we didn't leave. Slowly Lem became a person again, taking quiet gravel crunches over to the back of the truck to sift through the freezer until she found a cup of Italian Ice. She opened it and left it in the sun while she sat, legs drooping out the open truck bay. She was facing the water and I didn't want to be my usual self so I stayed in her periphery and ate a cone with crunchies on top. The wharf was empty except for us, our truck, and two old warehouses covered in green creepers.

I was about to grab an ice cream sandwich when Lem said, "*I used to eat it like this when I was a kid.*"

"*She sat there, legs dangling, not eating a thing.*"

"*Italian ice,*" she clarified. "*I'd let it get soupy and then drink it. Lemon was always my favorite flavor.*"

"*How was it having parents?*" I asked.

She warmed instantly but cooled her talk, "*Nothing special, Tag.*"

But I knew she played hide-and-seek with her words. Why wouldn't she tell me about it so I could pretend for a time? I pictured myself as a smaller me, getting hugged up by a Lem and a dad. Then we would have been driving past the Boy's Home to go to a restaurant and I thought it could be good to stop in and get a brother so I told them so.

"*Your parents loved you a lot, I'll bet, I said.*"

She didn't answer right away.

"*That's why you were such a good mom to Sam,*" I added.

"*No.*"

A slow-moving helicopter stalked a jam of ant-cars on the far side of the wharf before scoping the bridge, then us, until finally *sput-sputtering* off to someone else's life.

"*Sam died because of me,*" Lem said finally.

"*He lived because of you, too.*"

"*I didn't know he was sick. A mother should know when her son is sick. A real mother doesn't outlive her child.*"

If Lem kept getting torn like this, stinging and biting herself, Lem wouldn't be Lem much longer. I didn't know what to do other than walk over to her; let me get stung, bitten, torn.

I protected her from her flightless self with my arms and she pulled me the rest of the way to her.

I said to Lem, "I'm in love with you," meaning just "I love you," but instead I was saying *"Do adults still hug their mothers? Or am I a baby?"* the intended words rattling around inside until I was tingly with the start of tears ready to nip. I think Lem loved her mother, loved that man who left her and her baby, too.

"We're the same age, Tag," Lem said. She sensed my embarrassment and her muscles softened against mine and she added, *"Adults hug their parents, too."*

"I'm sorry about the ice cream truck. Should we return it now?"

Lem mumbled sleepy consonants; she wasn't ready for my questions so I settled myself down in her arms and we laid together in the alley of the truck, my smallness out-smalling hers, and I blinked a couple of tears onto her sweatshirt: a sweatshirt that might never get washed so my tears would always have a home.

It had taken a long time to be sweatshirt close with Lem. The day we met I had eaten pencil shavings; I mean I was hearing death groans; I mean, echo pangs; that's empty-stomach sonar. It took her son Sam dying before he could barely walk.

She cried as she fell asleep. Sometimes it hurt like starving to hear her cry; I kept still and listened to her chest storm under my head because I was unsure if she had crossed into unconsciousness, but this time her crying lulled me because I knew the difference between a full cry and an empty cry. She didn't sound like a waterfall in front of a cave: bad simile. She could have been that setting sun belly-flop-splashing into the ocean so hard Sam would've known it was for him; full-sunset so peaceful I feared she'd never want to rise.

When she woke, I was already staring at the high ceiling of the truck, wondering about why ceilings had to be so high in buildings.

"I'm going to get a job, Tag. And then a place to live, for us to live. We need to see about getting you some government assistance."

"What kind of assistants? Some Seeing Eye cats for when I want to save calories walking eyes closed?"

"I'm sick, Tag."

"You just need some orange juice, like you gave me when you were nursing me up."

"It's not like that."

"What's it like?"

"It's like getting older or like needing to sleep for a long time. I can't cure it. The doctors told me when I was having Sam."

That night we returned the truck and suffered a far walk back to our usual spot central to most of the *Calorie-Marts*. I looked behind us at the trail of calories we were burning, feeling my needle pulling toward *E*. I started walking like a tin man in some movie I watched through a *Non-calorie Mart* window until I had been asked to be on my way.

To where?

"I'm rusted, Lem."

"Bend your knees when you walk, Tag," she said.

"I know. Sometimes I just like you telling me things."

We crossed an intersection that reminded me of the day she went shuffling into the road, when I dove in front of that taxi and got smooshed to pieces and some garbled words *tick-tick-ticking* like a sprinkler. But she had said, "Shh," and later, "that taxi was meant for Lem, not Tag. It was my ride to Sam." She had cried lemons and they stung my cuts, but she stayed and cared for me like she'd tried to do for Sam. I remember the first days of recovery, in a bed that smelled like citrus. But before I was able to stand on my own Lem told me her money was dried up and that we were going to be evicted, which meant we had to leave. I was always being evicted from hubs and stops and public places and places that I hadn't even stepped foot in; anticipatory evictions. She moved us between shelters, carting me in a wheelchair I know she stole. There were nights when cardboard limbs were home. And during that time, Lem survived on my survival. Keeping me going kept her going, I was sure of it. She stalked Phantom Food for us while rat gangs stalked my dreams. They chattered vicious rat-things and I yelled, "Get off my stomach!" and they kept chattering until Lem came back. She'd said, "Shh," and the world landed its planes. She fed me like mama birds did.

"Another feast! I yelled. If this is the magic of jobs everyone should have two or three!"

"People need to sleep. They need rest," Lem said, sliding into our storage unit with a bag of smells that had me growling.

"If we feast like this every night, I'm going to forget all my food memories."

"Tag, I'm feeling weak."

And Lem's legs, like foals and babies and pups, just jellied out from underneath and she melted to the floor.

"I remember the way to the clinic, I said picking Lem up." She was lighter than her Calorie-Mart uniform let on and I ran when my legs would let me because I didn't know what was wrong. This is how parents feel when their kids get sick, and for the first time I thought of myself as a dad hefting little-Lem to bed.

"She's feeling weak," I said to the doctor, just as Lem had said it to me so he would understand what I didn't.

"She is going to stay the night. Are you family?"

I nodded.

"What is your relation?"

"Family, I said, saying I said by accident."

"You can register at the front desk."

"I'm going to stay here with Lem," I explained carefully.

"Everyone has to register at the desk, I'm afraid," the doctor said. He was kind but there was no wiggling away from how his words were wrapping around.

I took steps out of the room, looking back at Lem asleep in a comfy bed. The doctor led me to the front desk, twenty steps from her bed. But at the desk the lady was asking for my name and it wasn't the right name, *I'm afraid,* and I tried another and another but none of them were making it into that book of hers and they were talking about evicting me so I thought I should tell them that I got government assistants instead of a job which was okay because *jobs aren't for everyone* Lem told me.

But in the end they walked me another one hundred and thirty steps to the front door, that's one hundred and fifty steps from Lem. And I didn't want to return to our storage unit and chow down on the remains of our feast. I wanted a food memory of lemon ice and snugging up with Lem in that ice cream truck. So I hunkered down on the brick outside the clinic and did that old calorie saving trick, I closed my eyes.

"Are you sick?" a voice asked me.

I spent calories. I opened my eyes.

"If you aren't sick I'm going to need you to be on your way," said an officer.

"*I'm sick,*" I told him.

"*Then you should be inside.*"

Evicted.

I spent the night looking for a present for Lem, scouring the streets for the finest leftovers and came upon a full piece of chocolate cake, smooshed just a little but intact and without a single bite mark. The next morning, I walked back into the clinic and the receptionist let me wait inside until visiting hours started. I sat with the cake in a makeshift cardboard box in my lap, every so often checking to make sure that chocolate lean didn't finish toppling over in fatigue.

Sleepy cake for sleepy Lem, I thought.

The receptionist let me in five minutes early but made me write my name in the book. I thought I was going to be evicted again, but they didn't seem to mind my name this morning. But when I got to Lem's room it was someone else there. I walked back to the receptionist and asked her where Lem was.

"*This is her room,*" she said after walking me back to the same room.

"*But her clothes, I began.*" I didn't want to panic, but I felt my jitters prowling.

"*They washed her up a bit and put a gown on her. It's just until she leaves. We washed her clothes and put them right there,*" she said pointing to a chair.

They had changed her out of her only sweatshirt, the one with my tears blinked into it. They had washed her hair and she didn't smell like she should have. It smelled good, but unfamiliar. If it wasn't for Lem's face I wouldn't have believed that person was my person.

"*Can she come home today?*" I asked.

"I'll have the doctor come and speak to you when he is done with his rounds. Are you going to be here for a while?" she asked.

"Yes, all day."

"Good morning, Tag," the doctor said to me.

"Good morning, doctor," I mimicked back.

"Lem told us a lot about you. She is lucky to have such a great friend like you,"

"Family, I said."

"Yes, family. Tag, Lem is going to need to stay here. She is not feeling well. Actually, she has been sick for quite a long time."

"Did you try giving her orange juice."

"We will try that also. But I'm afraid that she won't be able to leave. I'm sure she will speak to you when she wakes up. You are welcome to stay through family hours. But unfortunately, you can't stay the night."

When Lem woke up she was her usual wind-tunneled self.

"They've got good food here," she said, so I asked her to give me a few food memories. It all sounded good but there was something missing.

"Tag, the doctors are going to come in with some papers for you to sign. It's for government assisted housing."

"To go along with all my government assistants money?"

"Yes, it's like that. You are going to have a place to live."

"When will you leave the hospital? I asked afraid she would say she couldn't, like the doctors had said she couldn't."

"What's in the box? A present for me?" Lem asked.

"Oh, it's chocolate cake. I found it for you last night."

"Did you make it back to the storage unit okay?"

"I spent most of the time looking for your present."

"You need to sleep and eat, too," Lem reminded me. *"Try some of the cake, and then I'll have some."*

I opened the box carefully and the cake kept its stand-ing-bit going. I showed Lem so the chocolate cake could be proud of how long it had managed to stay *cake*.

"*Looks good,*" Lem whispered. She looked ready to sleep again.

"*It's good! I said. Try it, I said!*"

"*You're right, it's great. An instant food memory.*"

"*Lem, how long will you be sick?*"

"*Not much longer, Tag.*"

She was crying a little and the sun was making her face a streak of sunrays. "*Sam, I love you.*"

"*Tag,*" I reminded her. She reached out and touched my arm and then slipped back and looked like that time we dropped an egg on the concrete. Bad simile.

I pushed hair away from her ear for no reason other than to be her mom for her, trying to say more than I knew brushing those strands away. I felt proud of myself for a moment, to be caring for Lem and to be Lem's mom.

I watched over her and watched over her, as Lem's mom and then just as myself; I'd never seen her sleep like that. I waited for her there because that's what family does. Lem had told me that after Sam died. The staff let me stay the night, but they said that Lem was going to be cremated in the morning like Sam got to be cremated and I asked if I could be, too.

They didn't know what to say. They didn't know what to say but their eyes were saying, *No way. Only Lem gets to be cremated.*

Then the doctor said, "*She has passed away.*"

"*Passed away,*" I said, thinking.

"*Died,*" the doctor wind-tunneled.

Died. But I just got to be a parent to Lem, just started being a mommy bird feeding Lem-chick all those delicious foods. I had no more to say, the nice doctor right in front of me quiet as I was, not saying a word, nothing thinking or saying a thought of a word. Is this how Lem felt losing Sam, only getting to be a mom for a short time? This is the reason for jumping taxis and firing all your government assistants and getting evicted because there's no home anyway when you lose your chicks.

GRACIELA

stumbling upon the second death at Michoacán Butterfly Reserve
*a Senor Raúl Hernández Romero y Homero Gómez González, defensores del
bosque yla mariposa Monarca*

Butterfly wings caused the forest to mimic
sounds of rain in a downpour of dizzying
synesthesia where a girl, unknowingly
a prismatic part of the whole, witnessed
the world: A face down body. Fungus
decomposing fallen oyamel trees before
termites. The scent of blood felt through
the fir network of roots. Sun congealing
blood-matted hair. Instinctiveness:
like rodents avoiding needles floating
in a puddle stepped in by leather boots
stained with motorcycle oil. Racing

My life that I forgot: the unavoidable
trash-smell I carried in my hair even after
using shampoos promising to suffocate my
senses with vanilla, forced into
maturing faster and choosing between
those shampoos I couldn't afford and the
insulin I really couldn't afford, born into a
system that made me desperate for
girls my age to not think any certain way
about me, yet hoping some boys would. I
forgot the word insulin even existed
because I was no longer Graciela of.

mice-hearts delirious with the feast of
butterflies up above. Milkweed poison-
filled Monarchs awaiting predators
that digested toxins: a black-headed
grosbeak shadowing the colony, snatching
nourishment, wind-shredded wing tips,
woefully feeding only herself, her young
perished in the nest with open beaks
from the increasing spring heatwaves.
A man, black boots. A hunting knife.

Michoacán, Graciela of scavenged soda
bottles: always drinking the dregs before
burning them for cash. That other little-girl
Graciela hadn't fled to Mexico without a
father who taught her to fly kites, without
a big sister still a better cook and
mother who invented fairy stories that
she was proud to boast to her friends about
and she still lived without seeing death in
Honduras on a farm with horses.

THE PLACES WHERE WATER USED TO BE

"Aren't you worried about California drifting out to sea?" Josh asks. Josh is the most boring person who you have to share your day with. He works in a separate division, thermal aeronautics, while you work in the hydrothermal aeronautics division. The joke at your company is that the *hydro* gets you all the funding. Though you don't directly work with Josh, he lives in an apartment building abutting your apartment building, and because you share a proximal living and working space you are friends; that's the way it goes. And so five days a week, and sometimes Saturdays, Josh folds his lanky frame into your two-door efficiency and manufactures conversation while his shaved blond head charges static against the roof's upholstery as you drive into the city.

"Not really," you say.

"Not really!? The Golden Gate Bridge will tear in half!"

"Then I won't have to drive to work."

"What about your wife?" he asks.

"She'd still be able to get to work, she works outside the city."

"No, Matthew. What would she think about California drifting into the Pacific?"

"Oh. She'd be really upset?" you ask, assuming he's looking for someone to give the correct answer, though it's only you and him in the car.

"That's right. Because she knows that most Californians would die."

He wants you to ask a follow-up question regarding that outlandish statement. Don't do it.

He rubs his head against the roof and then touches your steering wheel–bound hand with his finger.

"Did that *shock* you?" he asks.

You want to crash your car passenger-side-first into the bridge.

The car lurches to the right and your shock surpasses that of Josh's. Had you actually intended to crash just then, or had your hands just instinctually taken over? You slam the brakes; two cars up ahead have collided. Could everyone have crashing on the brain? A few cars continue to press forward and someone behind you honks. Your hands are shaking like guilty little boys and Josh opens his mouth to say something obvious when two more cars crash up ahead, this time on the other side of the median.

"What's going on?" you ask to confirm what you are seeing.

"I don't know. The Golden Gate Bridge is supposed to be earthquake-proof." Josh has figured out your situation faster than you. "Matthew, we have to keep going. There's room to get around that accident; see; where those cars are going."

You watch as cars snail around the two conjoined ones. The car directly behind you honks for such a long time that the noise dissipates into fog.

Josh touches your hand, no shock. He's sweaty and so are you. You need to start driving. Take your foot off of the brake and start to creep forward. Slowly.

Metal suspension cables wail like a discordant harp. You're barely even with the crashed cars when brake lights flare up in front of you. Wind dies. The sun hides at the precise moment the tension cables snap across the sky, as to give proof to pathetic fallacy. Look at how, like a little boy throwing a tantrum, the cables whip cars and smash concrete; you find yourself thinking, even at a time like this, you are glad you don't have children.

People scream. You can hear it through your rolled-up windows and over the sound of your blood thumping so hard it provides a bass line. Josh opens the car door.

"Close it!" you yell.

Josh obeys, but protests. He tells you that you won't get very far in a stopped car. He uses *we* when he speaks. He talks about being scared and uses *we*, and talks about calling work and your garden dying and somebody's cats until fog settles over the entire bridge. Josh opens the door again; thick fog plowing its way through your car. Brake lights dim. It's a sorrowful red-light district on the bridge. Screams quiet to dreamy cries as if the people had become babies fighting sleep. You don't even feel like telling Josh to close the door.

Josh is talking quietly about how you should call your wife. She needs to know what's happening and do you ever tell her what's happening in your life? He thinks she wants to spend more time with you. Dara, he speaks her name as if they are friends. How can they be with five days of long work hours and sometimes Saturdays?

Cars are screeching. Josh's door is slammed shut when your car slides into the two crashed cars which slide into the wall of the bridge. Cars on the other side of the street are piling into the median. Everything shakes. Cars are hopping, some off the bridge. The fog is rising into a sky that looks as stable as thin glass. Chunks of the Golden Gate Bridge are following cars over the edge. Yours hasn't skidded close enough for a view because of the two that you are pushed against; now one.

"We are going to die here! I always knew I'd die on a bridge," Josh screams. Voices are back, people screaming and cursing. Many cry and a few run for whichever edge of the bridge is closest. You're moaning involuntarily and, for the first time, thinking about Dara. In this moment, near what you think could be leading quickly to the pre-death moment, you feel for Dara something more than the marriage-love. You tell her you will have kids with her, will move someplace closer to her parents and away from bridges and you will research good schools. How Josh-like you feel in this moment, which makes you think about what Josh is thinking, about how he could be feeling these same things, and then your mind pushes further and drifts to Josh thinking these thoughts about Dara, not a wife of his own.

"Are you in love with my wife?" you ask.

"Of course I am," Josh says, through tears or leftover fog.

"Of course you are?!" you repeat. But what have you asked him? Have you confused pronouns, asked about your wife, or his, *are you in love with your wife, or my wife*? Can you ask again? The spontaneity leaves you and the car to your right, the only one between you, the walkway, and the sky, goes over the edge. Your car rests on the edge of nothing and one more tremor would send you easily over. Josh's door is closed and he's scrambling across you now, yelling at you to open your door and run. Others aren't running. Too much large movement: concrete, cables, cars. All being tossed around. Dead commuters.

"Dara hates her job," you say, grabbing Josh as he squirms across your lap. "And I've never really cared."

"What?" Josh asks. He's preoccupied with falling beams, looking up at them through the windshield, maybe trying to calculate their crash zone.

"Did you already know that?" you ask. But in this great panic hides soft moments of introspection. Josh is unknowingly given to his thoughts just like you were, and wants answers to the same questions.

Josh tells you, this is weeks ago, about the people who come to the bridge to jump. They hit the water as if it's land. The surface tension and speed create a—and here he makes a slapping—*splat* with his hands.

You pretend like you don't hear Dara complaining about the guy at work who steals her chair every morning, swapping it for his, or the woman who more than occasionally eats her lunch. There are more important things—like plummeting— why allow this preoccupation?

Josh doesn't want to die and he's letting you know. You don't want to die either, but you can't get in a word over Josh's adamancy.

"I can see over the edge, Matthew!" Josh says. Josh's frenzy makes you realize how much he loves life, his life. "If I die, tell your wife that I love her," he adds, facing the water, head pressed to glass.

"Tell *your* wife?" you ask. You are ashamed that you don't even know much about his personal life, how little you've bothered to get to know him. You promise yourself that from now on it will be different if you only survive, but are quick to reason with yourself, No, *I won't because I'm not really a caring person,* as if it's beyond your power to change this.

"Yes, please," he says, as if confirming. Did he mean Dara?

It doesn't surprise you that you aren't sure. You begin to assume that Josh likes his job more than you despite his division's lack of funding, or the fact that you know other guys he works with are constantly teasing him about, well, he's an easy target.

The earth quakes, metal from the bridge's archway rains, and the car starts to shimmy over the edge. Could a large enough earthquake swallow the whole bridge; and the ocean? It's a Josh-question. He's probably asked you this before. Does he speak to Dara this way and does she find it endearing?

You and Dara used to go to the beach at the end of Golden Gate Park. You used to yell over the wind to hear each other and when you couldn't hear, smiles on both of your faces spoke for you. Then skipping stones became part of your time there, quietly searching for flat smooth stones, showing each other before skimming them, unsinking. Then some days were too windy to go to the beach. Has the wind in San Francisco gotten worse?

"Matthew, we have to roll down the windows!"

You question him about this: why at this juncture do you question him?

"If we don't, we'll get trapped in the car when it starts to sink," he says.

Sink? You haven't even fallen yet. Concrete. Air. Water. Submersion. Josh is mediums ahead of you.

You're watching him kick out the windshield and it strikes you that you're watching with jealousy.

"I'll pay you back, promise," he says, crying wildly and stomping your windshield with both feet, slumped down in his seat for leverage. You're taller than him for the first time on a car ride and you notice that his hair is thinning on the top. His movements, or is it the earthquake, rock the car off the side of the bridge. Josh sits up in his seat, gripping the sides while the windshield slides down the hood in one spidery sheet. You fall, turning car-nose-first into the dive.

Tears protect your eyes. Josh is yelling, *this is it!* The speed plus wind is incredible and you are gripping Josh's hand, needing human connection; your hands have instinctively done this. Blue, turquoise, green, brown: you can't clearly see what's below because of how your eyes have blurred. You are *feeling* so much that it takes your breath away. This, you know, is directly related to feelings and not the fall; the swelling of love for your wife, of compassion for Josh and a sudden desire to hug him as you fall. You are Josh, his eyes and tears, his blurred eyes and falling-upward tears, and you say, "I can't see the water!" but are unable to hear the words, the speed is just too great and your voice is ripped from your mouth and violently whipped behind the car like a scarf being torn to shreds. And the fall from the Golden Gate Bridge could possibly take a minute, maybe two, so you aren't surprised when you keep falling, blurry muddy light-blue/green/brown below, the death rush heightening everything, shortening time. You, Josh, check your watch that you can't read at such speeds, if only you hadn't kicked out the windshield—*but it was because we were sinking, Matthew, or are going to sink*—and in your last minutes for thinking about your dying garden, you have thoughts of your coworkers which morph into your (Dara's) lonely ruminations about past friends and parents you wish you lived closer to, and the shame that inhabits you (Matthew) when you're suddenly able to see how, little by little, you've been accumulating isolation and infecting others with it.

Suddenly yourself, *just* Matthew, consumed by new loneliness having been separated from that previously intermingled thought, from Josh, Dara, and even Devon Turnball from the hydrothermal mechanics' division, who you know has to cross this bridge to get to work because you are often finding excuses for why you can't give him a ride. And for a moment you are fully aware of being only you, if for no other reason than for having thought, in the most incredulous manner, *I can't believe the fall is taking so long.*

The wind tears apart more of Josh's words, your ears grabbing the tatters, "believe!" and then "die!" We are all going to die; Josh is grabbing the tatters and you are yelling, "I can't believe I'm going to die!" But why can't you believe it? What about your life screams, *live?* Nothing. Your final moments are wasted in commute and you wish you had said something to Dara, told her about your feelings for her, because it's just dawning on you now to think them. She couldn't have known, always missing her lunch and missing her chair and missing her parents, and missing those words you never spoke. Josh says something that sounds like, *It's been ages!* The fall? His crying? Being face to face with himself? He could be referring to anything now but you know exactly what he's feeling.

"What makes you want to live?" You feel as if a correct answer will save your life, let you land safely. But you haven't just thought these words, their Dara's and they come from the shore somewhere below where you were skipping rocks and talking about the future, before the wind in San Francisco got too loud for words. *Answer her.*

"I love you," you answer. You know those words alone won't fill so much silence, so you decide you'll tell Dara about how she's sitting in the back seat not quite giving birth but crowning way faster than she should, hospital still a mile off from the looks of things, and then about your daughter in your shared four arms like a cradle and your quiet world banished for good; but more importantly how you are so happy for it, for the warmth of rooms filled with words: fights, whispers, and even cries that should have been there all along because you and Dara have more in common than most people and you even love it when she tells terrible jokes in the same way you've come to admire Josh's and how he doesn't flinch from saying five honest thoughts for every trite one and not vice versa. You tell her that she will find a better job, one without chair and lunch thieves, that's closer to her family because you think that you can find work there. There's doubt and uncertainty, like that time you were falling from the Golden Gate bridge with a former coworker and you couldn't work out where the bay begun or how you survived. You remind Dara of her intelligence and compassion on the days she forgets and she makes you feel like the world, as everyone needs someone to diffuse their small orbs of doubt.

You should definitely have hit water by now but the medium below, water or land, hasn't changed and doesn't look any closer or farther away. Josh is done crying but his eyes are as blurry as yours so he can't tell you where the water is or where it should have been.

DELIA

A QUORA query posted by User Delia (series of found stories: credit to the drivers below): "Need a change. Want to see the country. Can you make a living trucking?"

Paul Stockley, "I drive. Cl 1,2,3,4,5; D,P,F,T; B-trains; tankers; semis; truck 'n' trailer

I like it, and I'm not answering for people who drive trucks around cities. Firstly, a driver has to like driving. It goes without saying, except that folk seem to forget that drivers like driving. And it's almost genetic. I reckon that if you are a driver, then as long as the picture in front of you is moving, all is well with the world. If the picture stops moving, stress starts to build. What do I like about driving? Remember, I'm in rural New Zealand and we don't have much in the way of motorways or whatever.

I'm driving so much down on the Aria Valley road, delivering structural steel, "hobbits down there," they say, but I'm glad about that, a lot glad. Not the hobbits, never seen one. But the roads. Most of my roads are one lane in each direction with very occasional passing lanes. I do pull over from time to time to let folk pass, but I'm happy when drivers behind notice that I've moved left, coincidentally, just when there's a long stretch of straight road and no oncoming traffic.

I might do three-day trips max, coz you run out of places to go after that. It's nice to sit high on the road, and it's nice to be pushing 15&½ diesel litres and 522 horses around. That's one normal suburban car engine per diesel cylinder. Funny . . . I see flash cars with high horsepowers, and wonder where all their horses go. Generally, though, I do linehaul. Overnight, to the main city and back. Seven hundred kilometres, thirteen or fourteen hours, five days. I get home every night . . . um, actually, I get home at 5am, to sleep. Doing linehaul I take a very good frozen meal up with me. By the time I arrive it has mostly thawed, so 6 minutes in the microwave while I wash and make a coffee. My main meal of the day is away from home, so I don't mind spending extra to enjoy a reasonable, tasty, always-different meal with veggies.

(Thanks to the folk at EAT for their XL and excellent meals!)

I drive both 'cab-over's, the flat-fronted windbreaks, and conventional trucks with bonnets (hoods), in either articulated or b-train configuration. The artic (semi) carries a forty-foot container and makes up a 18–19m combination, the B-train makes a 22m (just over 71 feet) combo. B-trains corner better (the trailers follow the path of the truck much more closely than a long artic trailer), but the tails of both b-trains and artics can disappear out of my mirrors when cornering. Most of the semi-trailers I haul have quad sets (four rear axles on the trailer), and to aid tracking around corners, the rearmost axles steers too, pushing the back of the trailer toward the centre-line of the road. Without self-steer rear axles, the trailer would 'cut in' on corners and, on the tightest corners, would climb into the culvert beside the road or up the embankment.

I really like piloting a monumental vehicle around. Especially on our roads. Through intersections. Along rural roads, country highways, the flasher roads and the little bits of motorway. Heavy loads are fine. And gorges! Long but not high, fairly winding, bare rock tunnels, and roads that climb small mountains on just the same path as the 'winding road' sign paints. Cruising through a bare-rock single lane tunnel piloting a Western Star, nothing better.

And in particular, I'm very lucky. The two hours of road that I travel most is the bit I love the best. Close river valleys, pasture and bush. Gigantic rock gardens. It's different every day, and every day it's stunningly beautiful. Once I watched cloud falling off the top of a cliff onto the paddocks below. Into a slight onshore wind, looking all to hell like a slo-mo fluid dynamics demonstration. Another time there was a group of four quite young bullocks, chasing several seagulls across the field at top speed.

Keep this in your mind though. If you are driving a manual, you've got to like changing gear. I have 16 to choose from, usually, and getting through them nicely all the time is a pleasure. As is smooth braking. Though an auto-shift gearbox can be a nuisance if you leave it to its own devices, it'll plough through way more gears than you or I would use and be more economical than I would in doing so. I'll lay you fair money that much of the perfect shifting you hear on the road is a computer controlled synchro-with-clutch setup. The computer even double-clutches perfectly on downshifts. Though I admit to enjoying cruise control at times. (Cruise on trucks has control of helper brakes—exhaust brakes and the retarder for me—so is a fairly reliable speed management tool).

There are places I drive through countryside that looks just like Windows XP default desktop. Elsewhere I travel through nutso primordial forests (trees that look like Seuss drew them) or tree-fern stands. I follow one river from source to sea.

I also like dealing with occasional repairs and finding my way into and out of towns new to me—though it's suddenly a lot less fun when you miss a turn. You can't pull over anywhere and you are never sure whether you are about to find yourself in an annoyingly tight spot. These things do not do u-turns happily on city streets.

What's it like truck driving, you asked, Deli . . . I'll have to think about that.

Here's parts of the job that people might not think about:

You are never sure if the vehicle you are driving is going to be stopped, inspected, and a fault found. At a thousand kilometres per day of high speed driving, tyres die with monotonous frequency. In the middle of the night, the tyre service might be a couple of hours away from you. Adds two or three hours to your day, perhaps once a month—the semi I drive most has 20 tyres.

The vehicles are long and it's necessary to keep an eye on the distant end. You're supposed to know what it's doing. That means ducking and bobbing to catch the right view in mirrors, particularly at intersections where you have to be looking everywhere else, too. Cars can get themselves stuck in funny places. Such as under your trailer, or the truck's passenger side mudguard.

You can never, ever, park where you want to.

Soft-wall box trucks ('curtain-siders') are filthy. You're pulling and pushing a material that really loves road grime. I don't, so it's a point of friction between me and those trucks.

Cussing fuel gauges. They seem to have a lifespan half that of the truck on which they are mounted. And they don't just stop working, they go wrong and misreport.

Suburban traffic on Saturday mornings: Oh my. Oh. I mean fer [whatever]'s sake. Blue car below me, what are you doing!

Road signs. Please road authority, I need to know which lane to be in. And a bit of notice would be useful.

Mr Roading Authority, if you get both of those wrong, I can't make my way through your town. I can't make my right turn because I didn't know in time and I'm in the wrong lane. Now what do you want me to do, Mr Roading Authority?

And I bet you don't have signs that tell me how to get back to the turning I just missed. (Dear Deli, you may substitute Ms GPS for Mr Roading Authority, they're closely related.)

Oh, and trucks without air suspension. Jarring.

Rain. I don't mind it but it can, and does, slow you down. If you drop 5km/h for five hours, you'll be 25 km further away when otherwise you'd be somewhere else. I know what I mean.

Constantly watching for cars who will misjudge where our paths will intersect. They just not used to the idea of a long vehicle. A concrete example: The light is well green, the intersection is quite clear when the cab of my truck enters the roundabout. Because I'm turning I'll be slow and wide. It's going to take quite a while for the back of the truck to clear the intersection, Mr Car. Nothing will make it faster other than me shortening the truck, and I have a problem with that.

Cyclists of either preference: Eek, you're so squishy, please be careful. I'm doing my best for you.

Stopped school buses: I know the law says I must drop my speed from 90 km/h to 20 km/h as I pass you, but the law provides me nowhere to drop that spare 70 km/h. I'm trying. And the cars behind are learning.

Radio isn't enough to keep me amused during a drive, so at home I have a pod-catcher set to keep me up-to-date with a broad range of feeds, and regularly transfer podcasts to my phone. I get ten hours of listening time for radio and podcasts, so I enjoy a lot of talk. And I really do enjoy it. My phone bluetooths into the truck's car radio or plugs into an aux socket. Good sound.

To conclude, try a test run with someone who'll let you hop in their rig for a haul."

David Wright, "lives in Fort Smith, AR (2017–present)
We can and we do, some of us for much longer periods of time than others.

When I first started driving OTR (Over the road, you know it as "Long Haul") I put everything I didn't need on the truck in a storage unit, opened up a UPS mailbox near my home terminal and gave up my apartment. I don't have a spouse or kids or anything so I didn't see any value in spending $600 a month for an apartment, plus utilities, that I might only use for 3–4 days a month. I can get a nice hotel room just about anywhere for less than that. I lived like that for about a year and 9 months with my mother (whom I take care of) living on the truck with me as a full-time passenger. After that period of time she didn't want to be on the road for another winter so we got an apartment. I still take care of her but it's definitely more expensive as we had to buy a car, pay rent, electric, etc.

Many OTR drivers have power inverters in their trucks that allow them to have a small (dorm size, sometimes smaller) fridge, microwave and various other small appliances. I for one have a dorm fridge with freezer, microwave, instant pot, electric skillet and a toaster oven. I used to have a small portable propane grill too. A lot of us also have laptops, TVs, some even have satellite systems. so food and entertainment are covered. You probably already know this but we have a whole area of the truck that works as a very very small studio, minus the bathroom (although some trucks have those too, the extended sleeper trucks, they're very expensive though). This "Sleeper" area gives us a bed and storage for our stuff.

I still pretty much live out of my truck, but for short periods of time. Unless I happen to be passing by home anyways, I usually stay out on the road for 3–4 weeks at a time. Some drivers are known to stay out for 2–3 months at a time, some longer, some much shorter than me. it just depends on your needs and desires. There are some drivers who want to be home every weekend and while it is possible, not so much for the OTR drivers, they're better suited for a regional position or a local driving job. A big rule of thumb to remember, if those wheels aren't turning, you ain't earning. so the more time you take off (at home or on the road, aka a 34 reset), the less money you make."

Thomas Perkins, "Truck Driver (1996–present)

Yes we do to a point, I've been trying n the road for approximately 5–6 months with this latest company due to my Mother's passing last year I have to work hard as hell to relocate all our stuff to Texas which ain't easy bud I'm in my 50s.

Although I have 21–22 years of experience and love what I do to the point of being a workaholic always have been since I've started trucking lately I feel the burnout creeping up on me slowly but surely and will end up taking time off as soon as I leave the current company that's contributing to my burn out for legal reasons.

I've adapted to the small space inside my truck as best I can and trust me. Freightliner Evolutions are small inside compared to many high end trucks. I don't have a toilet sadly. I use bags and paper towels and I mainly try to use the bag when I'm not planning to cook. I have too much self-respect to use baby wipes and or a towel to spruce up and so I play in the water as much as possible when I get to a truck stop. I have a stove that fits in suitcase and a 40-quart cooler and a small freezer and three little cabinets for cans and spices clothes etc. Washing dishes is a pain and costly because finding clean water is high I don't ever use the water on the fuel islands, too dangerous because guys fill bottles up with various chemicals. Truck stops have washers and dryers and so no problem there unless they aren't maintained.

Have a few back issues from sitting but it's all good because I have a stepper to work out on and it feels great to finally tone up and start losing weight.

After a while you begin to notice the world pass you buy and you eventually realize that you are a slave and sometimes cry because what cash that you make goes back home to support your family that's getting older in a house that you hardly sleep in and one day you wake up and say to yourself that you're going to take your life back and if you're like me and fall for one of the traps created by Uncle Sam and start using a

1099 you realize that you may never experience a normal late ever again and so you become bitter at times because of isolation much like a prison on wheels it doesn't show every day but you feel it spike from time to time.

Eventually you don't even think about sex because having kids is a no no for most drivers because most relationships end in a bitter divorce and you work so hard what's the use in thinking about it?

The only option left is to try to go to some type of school and try to learn another career but by then you'll probably be old and gray and still stuck in a truck hoping that lottery ticket will be the ticket out your little prison on wheels.

Trucking is a career that has a glass ceiling that's thick as ice in the Arctic areas of the North Pole and so we're forced to live in trucks be it local, regional over the road you will spend more time in a truck than your home that is (IF) you still have a home by the time trucking gets done with you.

Living in a truck is a bitter sweet, yes we can live in a truck but there's a huge price to pay, physically and mentally and to a degree spiritually and you almost daydream from time to time of the day when the missiles fly and the world will fry.

Hey enjoy the stuff we brought ya for because we sacrifice a lot more than many veterans because we die at a rate of 3,000 to 5,000 a year and never receive a twenty-one-gun salute let alone one even though we serve our country too.

Never a Medal of Honor and hardly ever a decent funeral many have had to get back home in a reefer when they die because many of us have no life insurance whatsoever.

Live in a truck??? I just wanna live!"

Trevor Ray Slone, "Marine OTR Truck Driver

Please read comments and responses below. Lots of similar questions. Also, I'm going to add a photo that I took today in case anyone is wondering what I look like. I'm stopped in KY for the day and it's time for food and xbox!

Absolutely. This is my current sleeper bunk setup. A 50 inch 4K TV, a 5.1 Dolby surround sound system, a microwave, top and bottom bunk, windows that open and close with shades, cabinets, drawers, shelves, and more. And I have a custom Xbox One X, 5 TB external hardrive, and my brand new $497 fully customized Xbox Elite 2 controller and case. It stays in the top drawer when I drive but keeps me company elsewhile. I also keep my weights, bench, jump rope and bands in the truck, and pull them out to workout nearly every day, often while overlooking a gorgeous sunrise. I also keep my foldable $350 magnetic exercise bike strapped up on the top bunk with my weight bench and my bin of clothes, since I stay out a month at a time usually and sometimes it's too rainy or snowy to workout outside. It fits perfectly between the front seats, just like my $250 gaming chair that I sit in to watch TV or play xbox.

I keep my house robe hooked up near the top when I'm not wearing it. When I'm done working out for the day I put everything away and strap it secure. My space is neat and tidy.

The company pays for the truck, the maintenance, and the fuel. The truck runs on 180 gallons of diesel fuel so keeping everything powered and charged is easy, costs me nothing, and the truck even has an APU unit and this company let's me idle the truck all the time so staying cool in the summer and warm in the winter is also not an issue. If you want to see America and save over 95% of your income while doing it in style, this is the life baby!"

Theresa Atkins, "the Great White North, 7 years and pressin

Been running line haul through the swaths of flat scrub east of Missoula. Main complaint I have is the wind, whipping back against my cab, destroys the fuely bird pointing toward E. I think most truckers will tell you about the fight against E. Cuts into your time, specially when there's a queue at the filling station.

My trainer was a women as well, got to look out for us. She gives a care about us running long hours in the winter months when daylight isn't showing until after eight and you're up wondering sometimes whether you're still driving at night or what not. Don't have a family, but there's always a mouth or two at the lots telling me I should "change careers," with a laugh, asking me if I want to change careers "with" them. But for the most part they are looking out for each other, women included. Run into some people doing couples-runs, and sometimes even I'm surprised that the woman is the driver, though there's way more than there used to be. You can make it good in trucking for a few years, maybe even a career, but I do some wondering when it's late and those broken white lines start to hypnotize the minds behind the wheels. That's when I know I need a doze. Probably a drink (energy fizz or a 5-hour) or two would put me right but my trainer warned us about driving in the red for too long. Can't complain though, tucking a little away in my boots for rainy days and seeing most of the northwest, even parts of Idaho start to look pretty good after windy straights of western Montana. Think you could do worse. I needed a change and I got it too, for the most part, only wondering where those miles are behind me from time to time. Mostly guessing myself when it's the same frozen dinner for a couple days straight, like why'd I do that, eh? But met some good geese out there, running those lines like me and yeah, it can feel like a community. Welcome."

AKIKO

sap.

Tekkan was not on the train, and in his reserved-seat slumped an air of absence so strong it took on a visible shape. I saw my ghost-Tekkan, wearing a hat that covered his ears, wide jawline framing lips always in the curl of a half smile. I was allowed onto the train before it departed the station, to where his seat left no impression of him. There would've been a notebook on the proximate seat as his only travel companion. It may've been blank, there may have been pages crossed out and left torn on the floor, the jagged edges a hurtful reminder of the snowy mountains he entered in search of inspiration.

He had not consulted me before departing, but his mood had soured everyone around him and I was happy to see him go. I hoped that his continued departure meant he was still ferreted away in those peaks, getting fat on poetry for a buoyant return.

"Tekkan will not be returning today," I said. It echoed back in the form of a question from the mouth of Mr. Mori. He waited for our silence to coax something more from me but I found nothing.

He put his pencil down slowly, looking at me with deep eyes that have seen war. I noticed he was editing one of my poems in lieu of Tekkan, in preparation for the publication of their literary journal's next installment.

"What can I do?" I asked, in vague implication of the work left undone by my husband. Tekkan and Mr. Mori had published much of my work. I took a seat beside Mr. Mori, pencil at the ready to help with edits.

"He may return tomorrow," Mr. Mori said. "Or even this evening. There are many trains coming and going nowadays."

I returned to the train station, offended that my presence was viewed as an intrusion, as if the only things I was good for were a few pretty words and waiting for my husband. Glum and cold, I wrote some poetry while trying to stand out of the way of people who absentmindedly commuted through the train station. Without a clear head, the words meant little on the page. I was angry that I resorted to writing poetry, the only thing Mr. Mori saw me for.

Upon running into me, perplexed faces of commuters returned from semi unconsciousness gazed at me vacantly, as I was apparently standing in spots that people trafficked daily. Aside from the trial and error I suffered in the invisible warp and weft of commuters, eventually settling in a small triangle of space bereft of flow, the evening was depressing and salient only as it pertained to hunger pangs. That I had not even brought an *onigiri* was due to leaving Mr. Mori's den in such a dour state, and I blamed him for it.

I stayed until the last train didn't bring back Tekkan and walked home through windy streets, hungry. Hungry and cold.

I lost the entire next day to the train station. I was a constant in the flux of people collecting and letting go of their relatives, standing in an area well learned the previous evening. I brought food and a book to read, an account of Mr. Mori's War Journal, in hopes that, by comparison, it would make light of my situation.

Instead, I thought about Tekkan dying, myself dying, Mr. Mori dying, my poetry dying, all of the people around me dying. And I began seeing phantoms of tiny deaths everywhere. I watched as people gave their loved ones to the train, all of the smiling, tearful, indifferent, joyous goodbyes. I noticed, how after people bid their farewells, there was inevitably a moment where they stepped back into the rhythm of their lives and forgot about the people they had parted with: tiny deaths. Had Tekkan forgotten about me in the same way? There were many times during his absence when he was not on my mind either and I pondered the possible implications. Did I love him enough?

The following days brought and took trains.

Mr. Mori suggested I visit Tekkan's family residence in northern Kyoto, not far from the mountains he set off for.

"And what do I say if Tekkan is not there?"

"That you are on your way to meet him in the mountains."

Mr. Mori was always serious, a retired army–surgeon general who repented with the pen.

"And following that?" I asked, no longer thinking for myself, relying on a military tactician to sort my mind and organize me into action. It was a fault of a society that raised me to think so little of and for myself, to rely on the men around me, and yet I blamed myself. Not only that, I awaited his command and knew I would obey.

"And following that you will take to the mountains."

quail.
Silk factories churned behind warehouse doors on both sides of the street. They could still be heard from the serenity of Tekkan's family's temple, where his father was meditating but aware of my presence. The snow was deep, silent, and if one could believe such a thing, warm. Finding Tekkan absent only emphasized that depth, and for the first time I saw myself returning without him and tried to believe it, only briefly, in order to feel whether or not I would be lonely. But I couldn't make it real. I removed my mittens and scarf, touching the warm blanket of snow, refusing to believe that this blanket could be a frozen colony of flakes.

Flushed and stung with cold, I called upon his mother in the main house. She greeted me, with my flushed face, and asked if I was pregnant.

"Should we be expecting Tekkan as well?" she asked.

"I am on my way to meet him in the mountains," I lied. My mother-in-law and I took dinner together; she explained that Mr. Yosano was preparing for a funeral. I choked on the divination of the phrase and quickly tried to banish the thought from my mind.

"A woman has died from smoke inhalation. She forgot to vent her room and the smoke from her *irori* suffocated her. There will be a funeral tomorrow."

"I will relay the sad news to Tekkan."

"And have him pay respects upon your return."

I didn't respond, not wishing to lie any more in the home of his parents.

With me was the name of the town he started out from, that and the tidings of a winter reprieve. Roads to the village were clear and I was able to make the walk from the nearest port town without discomfort. I met a couple cresting the mountain pass, the husband grinning too wide for speech, leaving the wife to explain his dying wish, "a market selling urchins on the other side, and my husband having never tasted their briny insides, wishes to in this life."

He smiled wider, if possible, at his wife's honesty, at the mortality implicit in the words, happy to carry that.

I continued to walk with the couple into the village of sea urchins. My silence was filled by their comforting chatter, with occasional lapses as I receded into myself, inevitably comparing their relationship to that of Tekkan and myself. Was dependence a form of love? Through sharing stories, laughter, our lives, did we arrive at love? If only I could weigh it, compare it, see it from outside myself. Upon hearing Tekkan's name, I returned to their trickling banter. The husband assured me that Tekkan would be in the village waiting because no one who tasted the shellfish ever left.

"Don't tell the girl such outrageous stories. She will think we have lost our wits."

In reality, the village was barely inhabited, though the people there had met Tekkan.

"He wrote this and we sent him into the mountains with food and newspaper-stuffed clothes for warmth," someone told me.

See the trees possessed
by wind like one forced to dance
at a funeral.

"It's an unfinished tanka," I said. The format of the words warmed me with familiarity and I had the brief thought that maybe that was what I was searching for, familiarity.

"I suppose," said the elderly woman he had stayed with. "The Japanese doesn't make much sense to me."

If Tekken survived the mountain, if he was being nursed in one of the buried villages that saw freedom from the imposing shadow only between the very few warmest hours of the day, how would I have reached him? Whether he was trapped in a village or in the mountains, it wasn't rescue I could offer. I could only identify him, find him and say, "There you are, husband." What could I even do on my own other than write poetry? What could any little duckies do but swim and swim looking for rocks to rest on? For a rock to nest on. Perhaps a duck could keep swimming her whole life, and be happy doing so. Fatigue from my journey had created a surreal dream where I lived without my Tekkan, simplifying our lives to ducks and rocks.

lilium.

In the mountains of Tottori, during a whiteout erasing everything I know as Japan, rewriting it into a storybook yet to have words, I follow a snowdrift and its shadow for the semblance of shape, eyelashes acting as awnings bowing under the accumulation of flakes. My voice papers Tekkan into savage air shredded by frost crows and ice feathers. The distant fire curtained by crystalized panes is a beacon not of refuge, but of my failure. Numb, achromic trudging. Negligible progress, even my stomach has forgotten how much time passes.

Color returns to my world. Back inside a stranger's mountain house with her fire licking my belly awake. So comes the thaw.

tallow.

The village's physician cuts a stitch of acute language from his mouth; amputates your left lobe, eardrums still sonorofic in mimicry of the mountain's collapse. Ungloved, he continues to inquire; he traces the bridge of my nose, the peaks of my cheekbones, the sweeping concavity of my gauntness, in pursuit of numbness. His fingers linger for milliseconds too long on my purple lips itching to snarl.

And I wish to be undesirable for a time.

I leave with the dead flap of skin still attached: a frostbitten ear, a dormant lump of tissue, no echo, no reply from the joints of Mount Daisen. My failure to find Tekkan doesn't surprise me and I know it won't surprise Mr. Mori, who banished me to the mountain in an attempt to manage me as he has to the rest of Tekkan's possessions in his absence: property, bills, job, land, and akiko, all stamped with the name Yosano. And should I have children, all stamped Yosano. My poetry, stamped Yosano: the one thing that was mine.

I stare into my vanity, to scrutinize the condition of my ear, but the doctor insisted on bandaging it and my long hair hides it well. I will cut it. I clench my jaw and my features lock, lips purse, eyes harden. I relax my muscles and crawl my vision over my body. Have I missed the opportunity to have children with Tekkan? The need to have purpose is violent and overwhelming. I think about my volumes and volumes of poetry, which I have thought of as children more than once, and I am devastated by how effete that makes me feel.

gossamer.

I return south through Osaka, avoiding Kyoto, and without

paying my respects to Tekkan's parents or the woman who died of smoke inhalation. From one hub of civilization to the next, I hire a coach in Osaka and head east toward Tokyo. The journey is long and unpleasant. I return to Tokyo, that growing void of nature, existing like a chasm I am only too happy to fall into.

Tonight, the breeze is warm and the balcony's windows are opened wide in invitation. Down in the garden, alpine flowers are fooled into blooming in bright moonlight and I feel my fertility peaking. A yearning keeps me awake and my mind, like mountain flowers too far from bees, hums along in the womb of a train to a web of destinations I can`t give name to. Each step the unsure last of a flight in the dark. Tekkan's ghost weight hibernates me as I preside over the confusion of flowers. I feel myself trapped within a chrysalis, metamorphosizing into something. From what, into what, I don't know. The change alone is what I feel and it's both sad and confusing.

I wait a week before I scratch letters out to his family members, explain to his father and mother that Tekkan is, I don't know where, that I have lost my husband or that he has lost himself, or that he might be dead now that I have waited days to send word, or that he may die at some point along this letter's journey. The letters are vague and artless, even the act of writing is sacrosanct, my abstention from poetry thus far an attempt to not be reduced to the one thing that seems to define me.

I cut my hair myself in unruly lines like I did twice as a child, so happy the first time with how it tizzied my mother. I unbandage my ear, and without my hair to hide it, there like a birthmark is the dead skin where women wear earrings.

A gardener cuts fjords into the dense pines now that winter is relenting in the city; I have requested art from him when simple pruning would have sufficed. He works unsure as to what shapes he should be cutting away, unsure as to what will be left.

I spend the entire day watching him work and he is aware of me (sitting, doing nothing). Should I return to the mountains, great general Mori?

The night comes like horses pulling chariots.

The morning but dust settling on a deserted battlefield.

blood.

A blood orange squeezes across a waste of sky swathed with the faded stains of previous days. Anger is beginning to well up inside me, that I should be so directionless without my husband.

vellum.

I live in a world full of partitions. I leave with money, with suitcases, and tell Mr. Mori I will return in a few weeks because I am too weak to cleanly break from anything, save for my legs possessed by a cacoethes to shatter glass doors and kick holes through all of the shoji screens that create multiple spaces in my house for me to be aware of my own pointlessness.

"A hina-doll needs her shelf." Shame and funerary words for the truth I bury within me. I live on passenger trains and stage coaches, headed north, the opposite direction of Tekkan and his muse-mountain. From the perpetual-motion machine, I churn through fields of blossomless flowers ossified from cold, dormant rice paddies, the occasional farmer stumbling over snow piles yet to melt.

I change clothes with the brashness of a street performer and people look away, showing their contempt by the angle at which they hold their turned heads. I clean myself with snow melt when the train stops. The scented oils I use choke fill hired coaches. The windows, when open, howl. The memories I have kept imprisoned in scent and sound and tactile sensations are unlocked like deluging ice shelves. I have transformed my life into one of transportation and sense-memory in search of, what?

heshiko.

Accidently spoke loveliness to my Tekkan in five-seven-five; now I'm cursed to bind rules into my words. I can't write in a journal without scratching for a better word, without ranking words and dissecting them for their sounds and implications; I'm evil. I welcome the interruptions of steam trains' rattling panes, downpours like stage curtains ending plays. And in the wings of my thoughts, I understudy a younger me who doesn't respect her elders more, or herself less, still unbound from suffixes and honorifics. She doesn't furrow over words that muddle meanings if only to sound ever more slightly like a song. My younger me floats away as I return to my vexation of trying to write my apathy with some pretense of art. I tug at her leg to keep her from escaping in her lightness.

Eventually the train lulls me into comfort and pulls from within me, introspections. Imperceptibly the train's sounds blend: chatter, people shifting for comfort, wooden doors clacking open and shut, the bump of luggage on racks, the constant grinding of iron against iron, until I can hear none of it and my thoughts surface like mice once the cats have fallen asleep. I would like to live like this, in a transient house full of strangers and their conversations that weigh nothing on my life.

The milieu around me are busy maintaining their pleasantly familiar sounds and politely keep to themselves. I dip my focus in and out to hear a family discussing dinner and the weeding of gardens. I have a thought to invite myself for seaweed dumplings, to try on their lives for a day or two. A family of four sitting symmetrically and talking dumplings, this will be stitched into my memory, such an unremarkable moment in their lives.

In my hands a halved persimmon, its star anise–patterned seeds peeking between orange flesh before I dig them out. And then the star is submerged into the temporary darkness of a tunnel. My persimmon reappears as we enter the valley. The scene, through the laced glass of the rolling locomotive, is of a parish cut into the hillside, with harvested rice paddies terraced against the still-green mountainside, and the forest looking poised to take it all back and erase their lives.

floriography.
A man announces himself to my right. He asks if I am a playwright, acknowledging my open notebook with his subtle eyes. Death clings to my frock, and he sings a few words. His stare pleases me, sharp intelligent eyes, so confident and oblivious.

Something possesses me to travel with this man. I part with a fair amount of my luggage in the process of touring with his kabuki troupe, writing song lyrics for despondent lovers and fearless heroes. How does the antithesis of my life flow so easily from my mind? I am drawn to this man's performance, his entire life in costume, his face painted even in slumber and reapplied to remove any blurring before dawn. His name is No, but his understudy confides in me that this is not his name.

"He is a brilliant performer," I say to his understudy behind the stage.

"He's not even performing anymore, I don't think. I've only been his understudy for a year but there is nothing to study. I cannot live in costume, nor do I want to. How can I learn from someone who has no need to act?"

I prefer the company of the understudy, with his little dark pools for eyes, arms slenderer than mine, evoking willow boughs when draped over the pond of me. In his cot with swaths of sunlight framing our coupling, I take him under, still robed to hide the truth of my skin riding his. His name a secret inside me, a secret I am neither ashamed nor proud to own. He is not similar to my Tekkan, nor dissimilar, nor antidote or the cloud of unsettled solutions. He is he. I am still lost and I'm doing nothing to fix my directionless compass for now.

pith.

A new kind of routine has enstenched me in service of its numbness, a well-worn path of the itinerant. The smell of my indifference is masked by perfumes I wear as habitually as clothes, as a somnambulist haunts the same stretch of tatami, finding themself in the empty room of their ancestors when the undead dawn claws up out of the underground. Why can't I glean even a stirring of pain or mourning for my husband from the shelves of pages I have produced. My disorientation, once as deafening as the explosions of workers plowing tunnels into the mountains, wide enough to drive a train through her heart, is nothing but the incessance of wind, a background contortion of malaise, of bowls of soup untouched, steam dying like fleeing souls, and the miso a burial mound beneath a waveless sea.

I look upon the mounds of poetry Tekkan's absence has brought; enough to publish volumes. I spread the pages out across the tatami floor. I peruse the shape of their stories and smell their breath when the words whisper and ignite the fine hairs on my neck. I fondle their implications like a lover and tend to my fragility in the aftermath of reading back the pasts I have chosen to anchor. These moorings are not enough.

carp.

How will my story end, if not in a gentle crest of ennui?

kiln.

Though I don't know where I am—having traveled through hamlets villagers haven't even thought to name, having slept from time to time through entire swaths of towns and performances, and behests to wake and eat something—a letter reaches me.

swallow.

Bound to the name Yosano, I peel myself from my understudy, I move backward through myself, and will be dining at Yosano manor, with his sonless parents. Tradition will shackle me back in forty-seven days, in one year, and every year after, quicker and quicker as trains lose rust and wood un-rots and conductors and drivers grow young from victuals and powders.

It takes nearly two weeks of travel to reach Tekkan's family home. Silent the dinner I take with Tekkan's parents after the pleasantries. Formalities have dispensed themselves in glacial sheaves sloughing away to reveal more ice. Never aware of how much voice had been Tekkan's, how little poetry actually leaves my painted mouth, how little my lips are unpainted and I think back to my understudy lover and his mentor in constant make-up, talking to anyone he wishes from the malleability of a face no one gets to see.

"Do you intend to continue depleting his money searching?" they ask.

"I have not been searching," pounds against the inside of my cherry-unblossomming lips.

I am not the kabuki songs I have written.

I will make one more journey, fulfill my wifely duty and put our world to rest.

zelkova.

It is natural to write vertically, to see my characters falling,
to catch them, drag them up, and from those invisible white
peaks drop them again. I read their bodies, nodding as if
their meaning isn't a trail down the mountain, or dark
smoke
signals of insignificance marking the places I already
searched.

atrium.

A coach again to the villages on the outskirts of Mt. Daisen. And from there on foot. These are villages built into foothills and ravines, places that spend most of their daylight cast in shadow. A woman digging into the snow for root vegetables tells me that soba grows on the slopes and there are a couple of hamlets that grow ancient red rice," though now the terraced paddies cut into the mountainside look like a snowy staircase. The snow is deep.

Even on the main path wending along the river gorges through the villages. Could he have made it this far? I bring along the comfort of blank pages and something to write with. I travel with more bags than I should. They slow me down as I plod from simple inn to inn. I leave the largest behind as travel becomes more difficult during these waning but ever present winter squalls. I stay longer at inns than I should, but I'm afraid that exposure to the cold will lead to more frostbite and amputation.

amphora.

And in my extended tarrying, I resume writing poetry, more than I ever wrote before. I write like hyenas scavenging elephants, mixing meat with hide, sinew, tusk, and rotting organs. I lap it all, vomiting pages, never reading over any of it. I attempt to free my mind, to let it wander, cover any and all topics. But a theme emerges. There are birds. They sing. They twitter. They cry. They flee and return. There are poems that contain only wings. The precise beak of a green woodpecker. Boring holes. The stalking legs of herons wading in thawed rivers; nothing more than reeds to the fish that swim past.

And sometimes as I write I cry.

Whatever became of Tekkan I hope he didn't suffer.

I hope he found something meaningful here in the mountains.

There is still a slight nagging in the back of my mind. What will I do with the body if I find it.

In this village—which is barely more than a group of houses—the woman who puts me up for the night asks why I have come in winter. "There isn't much food. There isn't anything to do."

I tell her that I am looking for my husband and she furrows her brow.

"I wouldn't look for him here," she says.

I'm silent. She adds to her previous statement, the glitter of remorse in her words, she tells me there are only one or two more inhabitable clusters of life before the mountain itself.

I spend three days here contemplating my return. In my bundles of paper I find a letter addressed to me from Tekkan's father that I never opened.

The kanji characters are written beautifully and there is only a single, sparse sentence written on the parchment:

Do you want to find Tekkan?

I admire how much usable space he leaves on a page. The contrast of the dark ink, looking like stains on an otherwise clean sheet of paper. Each character carries so much more weight because of how few of them have been laid there.

The only thing I can think to do is fold up pages of my poetry and stuff them into an envelope. Leave it to him to understand my answer from all the words I have written. I look over some of my writing to see through the eyes of what Tekkan's father would read. He would find birds, murders and kettles and gleans of them. Solitary birds rooting through the receding sea shallows. Early morning calls that sooth the cicada's laments. Regurgitated worms into young bellies. Buffered down feathers shivering in the wind. Squawks over the crashing waves. Snake in talons. Fish speared in a beak. Black cormorant diving. Flocks of allusions and barely any white space where my characters don't cry.

I don't want to find Tekkan.

gorm.

Midmorning and finally a sun to thin the ice that has formed in a communal pool where vegetables are washed. I watch two women chip away, brief exchanges between them when they exhale. I am engaged in my undying habit of writing, using a pencil because my ink has congealed too much to use. I write while sitting on a rock that serves as the entrance step to someone's house in the most remote village I could manage to reach in the shadow of the mountain.

I am writing a list of my favorite words. It's calming to think in singularly pleasing bursts with no other context save the sounds they make.

I have nothing else to say, no reason to fill a page.

Tears stream down my face. I think this is out of love for Tekkan. A chapter, our chapter, has ended. I recall word-for-word poems I wrote in the throes of love, and these memories spill into remembering bits of my life with Tekkan. He used to read through my work like a gardener tending to weeds and gently encouraged what remained to flourish. There was always a lightness in my chest when my words were in his capable hands. I enjoyed watching his face as he read my work.

Suddenly there is an old man sitting next to me, possibly the owner of the house.

Suck yuzu, he says. He sits too close, breath terrible. I inhale rotting seeds. I inhale the color yellow tipping to spoil into some disappointment of green. His eyes are puckered like pickled plums, doubled red-setting-suns. He's staring into a pool of seductive slumber just beyond the horizon of his glazed eyes. He's tipping toward sleep, tottering with its weight but not able to fall. He's unaware of his boney leg rattling mine. Yuzu distracts you from the cold.

His face doesn't even wince, from sourness, from acidity, from the cold flesh

filling his mouth.

I do not take the crescent he offers. I do not speak, as is respectful. I do not shiver. He holds his smile long after the yuzu is sucked dry. His smile is a hole, lonely

are the teeth he hasn't lost. And then he pushes himself to a stand, bracing hands against legs and plods around the side of his house, pulls his pants down and pisses in the snow.

Steam and the sound of a trickling stream melting snow, sighs of an old man. I continue my list

eucalyptus.

plume.

silk.

cicada.

apiary.

phlox.

kismet.

sluice.

oasis.

ash.

papyrus.

balustrade.

Still occupying the front steps, looking out on the sparse communal space where women have since chipped through the ice and washed their root vegetables. There is a garden that has been cleared free of snow. There are footprints crisscrossing the snow on the sides of houses where a couple of people are bundled up and poking at the snow on their thatched roofs with brooms. There is a main avenue that has been shoveled free of snow, and it connects the cleared walkways of the houses in town. The sun has come out and the roofs begin to drip. In an hour or two there will be gleaming icicles.

Boys rush out into the avenue from a nearby house. One has kicked off one of his boots and hops around on the other, off-balance, to the delight of other boys. They dance around him to see if he will fall, taunting him into vertigo with their proximity. Just as he is about to topple over from the dizziness of hopping and spinning, a grown-up swoops him up off his feet in mock rescue.

It is as if the moment is created for me: the man, wearing a thick-layered haori, turns toward the world around him, the boy's hair wild in mid-twirl. The whole scene stops.

Boy in his arms, Tekkan and I see one another. He knows me instantly. His eyes still shine with exertion, and they are unafraid in their recognition.

His cheeks are flushed with cold.

He looks healthy.

He continues to look at me.

No time has passed yet. We are locked in an intimate recognition that ignites a panic within me. My heartbeat races. My mind is a blank page awaiting kanji.

The one-shoed boy wriggles free of Tekkan's arms and the youths disappear into the blurred periphery. Our eyes are locked long enough for conversations to play out. There is deep meaning within our gaze, but I am unsure of what we are saying. He is giving me ample time to approach, to question him, to allow him some admission of guilt, some explanation as to his existence. But I don't move. Neither does he, standing in the spot where the boys danced.

A lifetime passes looking into his eyes. The intensity grows to a point where I consider the deeper meaning of breaking his gaze. I can see it in him too. I can see that something significant keeps him frozen there, his eyes in mine. I see us returning to Tokyo, also to his parents, creating a family, writing cooking working doing being. Does he see our life as well? We continue to look at one another until at some point his eyes die in mine and mine in his, and still our gazes are unbroken. We will die like this.

All around us the activity of life continues.

My heartbeat and shallow breathing relax. Distant voices remind me of time passing. There is the crunch of a light creature in the snow above me.

I look up at a winter-fattened thrush that has landed on a steep thatched roof, feet and spindly legs disappearing into the white accumulation. It's too early for birds, I think for some reason. I follow the bird's inquisitive stare, to the snow-covered ground for seeds that will remain buried for weeks to come at this elevation. The snow is like unwritten paper in the places where people have yet to tread.

LOW-RISK ACTIVITIES

Graciela

Searching for drowned butterflies, I stumbled upon the second death at Michoacán Butterfly Reserve. And I started to run. My clothing comfortable and loose, my only shoes sneakers even though there was that hole emerging because my feet were growing too fast for our money. I was always ready to run and had learned it was better to run first and think later. I didn't like the adrenaline of fear, especially when I was coming down from it. Thoughts of cowardice. Being a girl, my poachable weaknesses. How often had my slender arms and legs caused my brother and I trouble, raised unwanted attention, those slender arms and legs that had already snapped into motion, running for *home*.

In that moment of fear I wasn't thinking that body face down on the forest floor had a similar brown park ranger uniform to the one my brother wore, the one they asked him to turn in when the *Parque Nacional Montana de Celaque* in Gracias lost funding for refusing to "cooperate" with the government, the one he didn't return but continued to wear long after we'd fled to Mexico, then Texas, then back down to southern Mexico to get some distance from Texas because Texas had been a bad idea, a real bad idea, it was the one he was wearing the last time I saw him which was earlier this morning.

Moments of fear rived me, her, Graciela. I became the whole forest focused into the present moment, and I became my own discarded skin.

I was running right for him. In another world it would have been my father, riding back on his favorite horse, all brown with a patch of white near the nose. My father liked him because he had tolerated the mischief of young children, myself and Luiz, without displaying displeasure. But there was no flannel up ahead, and yet my legs were ferrying me fast: jeans, shaved head, tattoos visible.

The butterfly-swirl that amassed in this protected biosphere was the journey of four generations, birthed and dying, across Canada, the United States, and Mexico. They were nomads too, wanders without passports or homes. I remember crying in truck-beds with friends I'd just made because I knew it meant we would lose each other. I listened and pretended not to when grievers mumbled their dirges for their murdered horses, stolen siblings and children, and skeleton-cattle with nothing to eat. I tried not to think about their deforested family trees, nor the branch my brother and I left behind.

I remember saying goodbye to my parents. It was the goodbye of a girl going on a trip with her brother, not the one of a girl feeling the flannel patchwork fabric of her father's work shirt against her cheek for the last time. But life had still been good before we fled, hadn't it? For so many nights after Luiz had shared the truth of our journey did I scrutinize my memory for horses looking too thin, for a missing calf in the shadows of so many in the herd, for less food on the dinner plate, in my mother's breakfast bowls. I would look down at my hands, pretend they were mamá's, and hold a nonexistent book in front of my face only to see the woven lines of my own story; were hers shaking in those final days of post resolution? I couldn't find the cracks I hoped for; we were broken before we were ever broken.

When I had left, I'd never said a permanent goodbye to anyone in my life. And since, I've lost every friend I made during my migration to Mexico. And every time I said goodbye, thoughts of my parents surfaced. To me, goodbye meant losing home and losing home and losing home and losing home and losing home. I never lost track. It was a final word so Luiz and I never said it to one another.

The oyamel's trees are sagging from the weight of butterflies that's how many clustering monarchs are dyeing the fir orange. Their wings still beat even after they have landed. That's exactly how I feel.

Foa B

This is my list so far:

An individual who fears the oven can practice turning on the oven for a brief period.

Likewise, a person who fears their house burning down can practice turning on the oven and leaving the house for a brief period, say an hour.

I can't be sure that this is safe so I'll run it by Michael.

A person who fears that broken glass has fallen to the bottom of the dishwasher can place a broken dish into the bottom of the dishwasher and then wash a load of dishes.

My side thoughts I allow myself to have because it's important to have an outlet for task-unrelated writing read as follows:

A person whose home is bombed can move to their other home. A person whose other home is bombed may—more thoughts on that later.

A person whose home is bombed becomes homeless, until they get another home. And then if they flee, they become refugees, even if they get another home.

Back to my first list:

A person who fears miswriting a check can purposely leave one letter out of the payee's name or out of the signature.

A person who fears making mistakes in conversations can purposely "misspeak" without correcting the mistakes. More generally, a person who fears performing actions imperfectly can purposefully build minor "imperfections" into every act during a designated exposure period.

A person who fears chaos or disorder, can make lists they don't use.

No. Michael would say they should create their own disorder, low-risk disorder.

A person who fears disorder can put a fork in the spoon rack and wait to see what bad comes from it.

A person who fears chaos can track a little mud into the house and let it dry there. Don't make your bed up in the morning. Put your pillow on the floor.

Even just writing about putting a pillow on the floor is exhilarating.

Mispair your socks, and if feeling incredibly bold wear mismatching socks in public.

This is too much. I am giddy. Will Michael use any of this?

Unbutton one button on a shirt if you fear, if you fear, holes!

No, *if you fear being untidy.*

I don't think my ideas are all that good, reading back over them.

If you fear inadequacy, write a book with another psychiatrist so you won't be judged alone.

I think I am only feeding into my inadequacy by crutching

up on Michael. Should I tell him I want to write this thing alone or not at all? I fear rebuke from my peers. I look out the window instinctively but I hate this view. I can't look at the Ouse River without thinking about Woolf going in and never coming out. How closely does having "a room of one's own" connect to a fear of being bombed at home, when your fears are *rational*? To have a room of one's own, four walls and a space that's yours, that you can just exist in without worrying about buttons and underwear, and then it's bombed (for the first time). Makes it hard to feel like it's "a room of one's own" when it can just be taken away. And then for it to happen twice! To cope with something like that you'd have to destroy your own home before someone else can, or take your life before someone else can. No, not that last part. That has little to do with the suicide of someone who lives with depression. But it can't help. Back to my list (the one I'm supposed to be writing):

A person who fears being alone can schedule short periods of alone time.

Note: ask Michael about people who fear being alone and *are* already alone.

A person who fears slipping and falling can put a little water on the floor at home.

That might be dangerous. I'll let Michael decide. They are supposed to be activities that people can do so they will see nothing bad happens. But doesn't something bad always happen? If I fear something bad happening, should I do something bad? Should I let something bad happen on purpose, within reason? Is this useful advice? In order to see it's not as bad as I thought?

If you fear something bad happening, let someone rob you of just a little money.

That can't be good advice. And it's a vague statement that doesn't help with obsessive-compulsive disorder. Bad things are always happening and everyone must fear that. I don't know why I came to the UK to work on this book. Even when I'm not looking out the window, it's the act of being here, in someone else's chair, sleeping in someone else's bed, eating off of forks that other people have used, that feels so inappropriate and lonely. Right now I'm sitting in the slipstream of so many thousands of previous guests. I should ask this B&B how many guests they've had. Maybe I'll feel better.

Bagman

I have a role and it's just to be here. Confined to living full-time in a three-inch space between the floorboards and a bed frame, I spend the nine hours Donny is away at daycare making lint palaces under Lincoln's bed or elsewise strain my eyes in residual daylight reading books scavenged from the house's library. But aside from pages, and distant voices not clear enough to eavesdrop on, and nightly laments I hear from those who live above me, my day is chiefly occupied with chronocide. With time to think and time to read I have reduced my life's search to two questions: What am I doing here? and Where is my home? I think I mean that I have reduced myself to searching for life, because I don't really believe that spending days trapped in this room constitutes *life* as humans use the word. I read about people having "purpose," and then I think about how mine is just to be here, under this bed, and I can't believe that I even exist.

But that is the point of me, to be under a bed, never to appear, but to give the appearance of appearing. Sometimes I purposely creak a floorboard, or bump against the bed frame in the middle of the night. But for the most part these movements are only a result of trying to get comfortable. I have at times reached my hand up the side of the bed and felt the plush down and soft padding that surrounds a bed. They are fearsome inventions. Without the antipathy of the hardwood beneath me, how would I ever wake up? Would I even want to?

I read stories about myself, me, who has never left the shadows of this framework, and burn with comradery thinking that there must be more like me, hiding under beds waiting for nothing. But that some of us have grown tired of being here and have ventured out, only to be trapped and vilified within stories. I have to mention that in these stories, it's never really clear what our transgressions are. We are akin to Kafka's condemned, imprisoned to the underbed for crimes unspoken. We are treated like we are irredeemably evil. We are treated like our existence threatens peace. We are treated like *sub*humans. And when I think more about my choice of words, I don't believe we are being treated at all. Quite the opposite in fact, specifically untreated.

Graciela

But where was Maria? She had come to the forest with me, camera strapped to her neck. Her camera looked a lot like my mother's and made a pleasant *click* sound when you took a picture. She let me use it after only a week of knowing me so I let her in on Luiz's and my way of making extra money; we collect recyclable materials and sell to the recycling centers. I told her this in part because I wanted her to understand why I always had the faint air of trash about me, as recycling participation is still quite low and some companies will pay for reusable materials if you don't mind looking. Maria wasn't my only friend here, but she had quickly become one of my best. Actually, I made sure to make friends everywhere I went.

White-and-black fringes highlight the orange monarchs, a warning to predators of toxicity. And they travel in large, poisonous-looking clouds.

With predators everywhere friends were essential. More than just splitting the loneliness, the girls I paired and foured and sixed with, always trying for even numbers so one couldn't be singled out, ensured our barely toxic selves would create one potent being to ward off predators. Even in Honduras, it was best to be a collective: to provide witness, to create a compendium that sorted everything and everyone into "unsafe" and "not yet unsafe." When *La 18* found rural Honduras with their "children's army," our parents warned us against making new friends. And when my father's ranch suffered at the high cost of their "protection fees," our parents asked the unimaginable of my brother, Luiz, to kidnap me away from Honduras.

Maria, I know, had never seen a gang member, but I told her what to look out for. Tattoos, expensive clothes, and of course weapons, especially if they were poorly concealed because gangs run the country and don't fear the police. And ahead of me were all the signs, including a dagger still wet that I was going to wish I hadn't seen.

Umbrella Pine

A seed scattered by the wind carries a universe. Like the comets that collided with this earth hiding organisms within water, seeds carry the promise of life, giant life. Even the sequoia began as a seed. Deep reaching roots that search for the origin of the earth. The ancient cedar of Japan's Yakushima Island, blanketed by moss and uncaring, for they have learned to live and harbor transient organisms throughout the eons. The aspen collective known as Pando has a root system that stretches back eighty thousand years. There are of course the young saplings just starting out, the fledgling mangroves that have just peeked their heads above water, the quick acacia in the Amazon will race skywards as soon as one of the older giants falls, seeing its chance to live in sunlight. There are so many trees on the planet, three trillion of us, three and twelve zeros, four hundred trees for every human. Before I even had a root of my own, I breezed through the air, having slipped from a prestigious and long-lived umbrella pine set high up on a hill. Because of my lineage I was choosy; passing up the banal clearing, overshooting the groves of cedar and cypress until I found a beautiful yard on the far end of the property containing a house with appealing matte-black tiled Japanese roof and gorgeous retaining wall that would protect me from the wind.

Sowing myself into the soil was more difficult than I had thought, as the place I had chosen to land had a wide rock just below the soil line. My taproot stalked along the edge of that rock for some time before finding deeper soil to dig myself into. But for the time being I had sun, solid rainfall, and protection from strong wind via the wall that lined the property.

I called it a blessing when the woman who lived on the property first came to nourish me with water on a hot day. Her husband, with two green thumbs, laid mulch around my sprouting self and protected me with a netting to keep deer from nibbling me to nothing before I was old enough to defend myself. And in this way, I was nurtured to great health. I had visions of becoming a great fat tree, a six-thousand-year tree, a ten-thousand-year tree with rings like water rippling across the entire Pacific.

But as I grew taller, the woman began to hunch and the husband stopped coming altogether. She offered me rotten vegetables and food scraps without properly composting them and I searched the ground for any mushrooms around to help break down the disgusting fertilizer, but I was on my own. Time passed this way, and though I showed my displeasure for her fertilizer by swaying even when the wind wasn't blowing, the woman was stooped toward the ground, not seeming to notice my graceful movements. As I focused on working through the rot seeping into the ground, some of my needles fell. I thought it might help to auto-digest some of my own needles, that it would somehow offset the un-composted material she kept leaving me. And when I finally got a handle on how to process the ooze she was quite happily bringing me, she began to read.

It is no secret that plants and trees like human voices and music. In fact, I love the violin. I could listen to it all day long. I often dream about being a tree in the yard of Takezawa Kyoko while she practices. But this woman only reads to me from a never-ending supply of crime nonfiction. My mornings are angelic sanctuaries where I dine on the dew collected on my needles overnight, savoring their essence while watching the mist burn off over the mountains. But now they are often interrupted by this woman reading to me about *tsujigiri*, killing sprees, lecherous solicitors and rapists, ultimately brought to justice, but that's not the point and its only half of the problem. She offers commentary. I am never spared her insight. She pauses from her reading about assaults and murder to mention how she doesn't know how she can keep reading, how she will faint from sensitivity, how her husband would have never wanted her reading such darkness. And she can't refrain from boasting about how she would have handled certain delicate matters differently, even sometimes chastising the criminals for not doing a better job covering up the crimes. I attempt to shade the pages with my shadow, or to allow sun to shine through my boughs and create glare on the words she reads, but nothing seems to deter her.

I heard a rumor that listening to human voices or to music is supposed to aid our growth, but I worry that this woman's reading is somehow infecting my roots and causing me to bend and twist as I continue my expansion. Worrying can't be good for my development and I'm already self-conscious about posture because I grew out and away from the property wall a little too eagerly when I was young in order to see the sun. It was a matter of poor planning, just like how I was less careful at that young age about where I allowed my roots to search for nutrients, because now one of my oldest roots is conflicting with the wall.

Graciela

His hearing was sharp and his vision caught hold of me before I could even change my direction. Don't look scared,

I told myself. If I acted like I hadn't seen the dagger he held half concealed at his side, maybe I could pass without problem. There was room to get around him. Did he have a gun as well? I needed to let him know I wasn't alone and that I was running just for fun, not from a corpse. I needed to do this all concisely and calmly.

"Great day for some exercise. My friend stopped to take some pictures, have you seen her?"

He shook his head slowly and began approaching, dagger concealed completely. I took in his stocky frame, his jeans, heavy boots. I could outrun him easily as long as my glucose levels didn't crash.

But then I saw Maria standing on the path behind him. I could see her and I could see that she saw the dagger the man had concealed behind him. She wasn't quiet and he turned to find her there holding a camera in her hands. He stopped approaching me. It was clear to him that Maria had seen the dagger, possibly had taken a picture of it. I wanted to yell for Maria to run but I wasn't sure she could outrun the guy. Who would he chase if we ran opposite directions? I figured it was her, what with the camera as potential evidence. I wasn't sure that she had the instincts to know just how dangerous this guy was. And she couldn't have known I'd just found a body further down the path.

She locked eyes with me, but instead of fear she seemed to be trying to say something.

Bagman

Where am I home?

I read about the Rohingya Muslims flung from Myanmar

like a bogey, fleeing with their bags on their heads. I'm reminded of reading about being called *el hombre del saco* in Spanish tales and *Torbalan* in Eastern Europe's: in so many languages we are the Bagman. And I wouldn't even have minded. There's nothing wrong with being a Bagman (a word significantly softened sans italics). Bags are useful. It wasn't until I was reduced to that one thing, an innocuous thing I never would have hated until it became something to define me. The Rohingya have come to the imaginary borders where they await being knighted as "refugee." I think I must be a refugee too, one that has forgotten where I have come from because how is it that the underside of a bed is both repulsive and comforting for the same reason.

Foa B

For people who fear rejection, try applying for a job you have no interest in.

That seems like a waste of time. I don't think Michael will approve of that one. For people who fear rejection . . . I fear rejection. What do I do when the fear rises? Well, I suppose I keep fearing it.

For people who fear rejection, try petting an uninterested cat.

If you fear having sex, just don't have sex. There's lots of other stuff to do. The world has enough people already for Pete's sake.

I don't think I can include this last one. And I should probably let Michael handle the subject of sex.

Umbrella Pine

She comes walking out to interrupt my bird-watching. I'm getting quite good at identifying individual crows. I am especially keen on one that drops offal from its beak while sitting on my branches. It's clumsy, but the decomposition offers enriching fertilizer and attracts mushrooms.

It's my lucky day. The woman is bookless. But from behind her emerge two men in garden attire like her husband used to wear. I feel them through the ground before they have even arrived at my trunk. They examine my trunk and roots. They follow one of my main roots across the ground, under the earth, and stop where I have worked my way under the perimeter wall of the property. They are examining the wall. They consult with the woman. She points to another area in the yard and they walk over to a spot where the morning light isn't quite as good and the ground not as shady. The men are measuring the ground and scratching their heads. Then they begin to dig a hole in the ground. The day has grown cloudy by the time they leave and the woman comes over to me and hugs my trunk for the first time since I've been growing here. Trees also like human touch. I like it so much that I would even tolerate her reading for daily hugs.

The two men are back the next day with shovels. They are digging a perimeter around me. I try to ignore them but they are irritating and their noisy presence is keeping my favorite crow from coming around. They strike and sever some of my fledgling roots as they get deeper. As they continue, I become quite unstable and I feel myself shifting in the ground. Where is the woman? Did she know about this? The sun is shining on my root system that works better when buried. I'm beginning to feel unwell and shed some of my needles for some quick nourishment. I can't help worrying as the crater deepens, because it is clear they mean to dig me out of the ground. They are careful during the entire task, leaving my roots fully intact except for where they have cut straight through the root that has nestled in the cool dirt under the perimeter wall. That was hard to bear, becoming detached from such a sturdy and fruitful root. Plus the loss of my fungal network, millions and millions of underground fungal lines that connected me to other plants and even trees as far away as the distant hill. I've been cut off. Will the isolation ever be repaired?

In a wheelbarrow, like some kind of thing, they bring me to the spot that they had measured out and dug yesterday. I don't like it. The ground is much warmer than I'm used to and the soil is devoid of life and information. They place me as gently as possible, and fill in the dirt around me, offering a healthy fertilizer that my remaining fledgling roots seem to like. But I feel sick staring at my home across the yard. It's just a hole left behind where I used to be and I don't want to think about how it's going to look in a year or two, will I even be able to see any indication that I used to live there?

Bagman

What am I doing here?

I didn't have an answer to the first question and this one is no different. Under this bed, in dim light, and often no light, I am thinking, reading, and listening. Sometimes I listen to nothing, just to see if a sound will come into existence. And sometimes I spend a good amount of time staying focused on a sound, the exact way it sounded, until I can't reproduce it in my memory anymore, or another sound replaces the one I had been trying to hold onto. When reading, I can ignore sounds entirely, when the book is good. I prefer nonfiction, or any book that does a good job describing the entirety of a house and home. It's odd to be in one all the time and not have any idea what it looks like. I think for that same reason I like reading about American history, as the house I'm in is something like a symbol of the country.

I have dreams about crawling out from underneath this bed and making something of myself but I don't really know what to make. These aren't real dreams. They are American dreams. And I am not even a real American so I don't think I would be permitted to have American dreams anyway, if it was even possible to dream myself as an American having dreams. How could I be when real Americans don't even believe I'm real. They can walk around forgetting that we exist there under their beds until they are so tired from making their dreams real and need to retreat back to their beds. I can't speak for other Boogiemen, but I like to wait until Donny is just about to fall asleep and give his mattress a nudge just to remind him that I'm there.

Graciela

Maria nodded to me let the camera fall so that she held it by its strap. She swung her arm back and then forward and released the camera high into the butterfly filled air. And in the moment when the guy's vision went skyward, trying to follow the camera's path into the frenzy of butterflies, she turned to dash. Without losing a beat I was skirting around his range of reach and trying to catch up to her. We ran together until I felt my body getting dangerously low on sugar and had to stop on the outskirts of the Butterfly Sanctuary, the man with the dagger nowhere. Getting dizzy, I told Maria I had to sit down.

She pulled a few sucking candies out of her pocket and handed them to me.

"I brought them for you just in case," she said, flushed and sweating.

"You remembered that I have diabetes?" I asked.

"Of course," she said.

Later I would dread the walk home, uncertain as to whether or not my brother would be there. But for the moment, I sucked on an orange candy with my best friend, who had thought quickly and could, as it turned out, run as fast as me. I hoped that I would never have to say goodbye to Maria.

Umbrella Pine

She has planted flowers in the place I used to live but the undulation of a hole is still there if you know where to look. The addition of flowers has brought color to the yard: an array of pastels, along with the pleasant buzzing of honeybees and the drunk flight of butterflies that I've grown as fond of as the crows. And still, it could never replace getting to be there myself. The woman, she still comes out to read to me, making me suffer through her crime stories and commentary, but she hugs me when she is done.

Foa B

If you fear having sex, just think about the eight hundred guests who had sex in the same bed you are sleeping in.

Eight hundred guests. The B&B I'm staying in has had eight hundred guests in the three years they've been open, at least that's what the owner tells me, and she tells me that's an approximate number. I really think she should have stopped having people when she could no longer remember each person who had stayed here.

I know I have a fear of being forgotten. I'm pretty sure that is why I'm writing this book, to preserve myself via my name because I never had kids.

If you fear being forgotten, try not having kids, try writing only one book that you're pretty sure no one will want to read and bequeath the copies you keep prized on your shelf to someone who you know will use it as a door stop.

There are people with lots of kids, with lots of books, and their name everywhere: carved into buildings, sewn into clothes, signed onto hats and books and boobs. And they have TV shows watched by millions with fan clubs and cults of people who would just die for them.

And then there are some people who come home from the UK to find their home has caught fire and burned down, and they make the newspaper and keep the clipping.

If you fear losing your home because you only have one . . .

Mastery of Obsessive-Compulsive Disorder: A Cognitive-Behavioral Approach Therapist Guide, by Edna B. Foa, Michael J. Kozak

HIFUMI

The bus takes me into a small town in Fukui Prefecture that looks unchanged since childhood, empty except for us by the time we reach our destination.

> The unpredictability of snow
> Cold fronts and warm fronts misaligning
> For the third year
> Now it's summer and the cicada are in heat

Water not locked in snow in the mountains, locked somewhere else, in clouds that keep missing the shore, dumping themselves in thunderous deluges off the Sea of Japan, within view of parched farms, but my grandfather doesn't cry. He complains about the population dwindling and pokes me to get married, have a million babies to replace the million babies not born last year.

> Maybe we are pregnant
> Clouds missing the shore
> Maybe we have yet to form clouds
> Still imagining their shapes

Tomorrow my grandfather dies. My tears are like saltwater. He wants babies, he wants rain, mountains pregnant with snow. He wants my grandmother to poke me in his stead until I burst. He wants to come back to life and remind me that he's one of a million people dying, not being replaced.

In this town they dig up dinosaur bones. Places that used to be hillsides, places that used to be homes, the earth is exhumed until the earth loses its earth and we are staring at a spot where we know an ancient being moved for the last time.

My grandfather wants to die out on his turnip farm. He tells us to leave him there so there will be some evidence of the millions of modern *dinosaurs.*

They're going to think we spent all of our time inside if we never die out here again.

I ask him who *they* are? And he tells me, *the future dinosaurs that will dig up nothing of us if we don't start dying outside.*

I say the future dinosaurs won't want to dig us up anyway.

At the very least, he says, *let me keep fertilizing my turnip farm. Your grandmother won't do it.*

In my dream, you and I are having sex in my grandfather's turnip field

I wake up and don't want to have sex

I'm relieved when archeologists offer to buy the lot

The bus swells with more and more people as the city returns. The news says we are a country of people who don't want turnip farms, but it's more complicated than that; my grandmother didn't get to decide, but there are millions of us now, city buses filled with women visiting the countryside to bury their ancestors and dig up dinosaur bones.

EURICE & AURICH

Aurich

Pull a knife across my swollen shuts. Listen to dawn fill the building's wounds. Wounds frosted and stained; a refracting blue robe corralling light into blinding slivers tattering his kingly raiment, some dark-green foreboding above the figure's head, barely a halo keeping the forest and its thoughts from entering the mind. Listen to the thickness light gets lost in. Remember. The thickness. for later, congealing blood-silence thickness. A Romanesque cathedral unplayed organ and Charlemagne asleep with stone eyes and a fake sword, red hilt. A thickness. Gold crown sinking his vision: Charlemagne who lost and found Aquitaine. Managing to lose an entire region of France while claiming a thirteen-year-old Swabian waif. Shivers. Little plots. Intricate piping. Power & Control demanding palanquins on each shoulder; no room for the devil. And where could the angel sit? Who will sing for his puckered ears if not the push-pull struggle? That hammered-gold crown looks lusty, like it would fit me perfectly. *Cumbersome, the color of gravity* said my partner, shrugging off the crypt as the stone steps regained their echo into the apse.

We walked the hall in an uncomfortable *stillness* she told me later had been *godsent*. The last two days' heat had *turned us piranha* she whispered over fondue neither of us ate. Swishing moist bodies through liquid cheese, pulling dripping white ghosts from pools to look at them with the pitiful knowledge that we wouldn't consume them. Back into the coagulating sea and the single ripple created by a slender neck pronging porous eucharist. *Turned me piranha.* I felt my teeth sharpen when I spoke. My silver forking stalked hers as I talked my way closer. I didn't like where this was headed. She had possessed herself of something I could never touch in the divine curvature of the nave that morning. In a geometry of shade that the architect surely hadn't intended was an altar.

Eurice

Wrap me up in bondages, mummify my thoughts and pores, seals jade and the skin we have stitched like accordions around a claustrophobic anus, *we can take more* it says, and my rectum is packed with scarabs' jeweled carapaces and wings, flight dime nickel zirconium. It's embarrassing. The pressure within & without stalking me into examining a small suffocation within glass; Was she human? Was she feline? Tabatha the only cat not bagged for the sarcophagus, Tabatha who had Mercury poisoning and Jupiter silesnia, Plutonium and Neptuned Rings cataracting her eyes, Tabatha who, as you might have guessed, has been blind since Saturn scythed Saturn's dark pendulum, Saturn with ringlets of her own: dark curls, icicles, slivers on which some-he savaged his gums as he serrated me, as I feigned awe, eyes desiccate and wrung from exhaustion, in an unremarkable space beneath three ribbons of stained glass, in each a man shedding his sins and bathed beautifully chromatic far above me, the cast-light kaleidoscope snagging high on a stone pillar: there was nothing here for me. There was an encased altar, conspicuous as the sole object in the nave, displaying a mummified creature so shrunken from existing that she was no longer the size of her wrist bone.

NESS

Your father's will: an invitation to a funeral and an invitation for everyone to leave with items of interest.

Already relatives talk to one another from the proximity of their desires.

He's your cousin's 'ousin's 'sin, so distant you could marry 'im; wearing black as a statement and mourning for ratings. How does something as inconsequential as a lobe attract so many holes? He finds a coalition of distant relatives like sharks in parts per billion, talking about death like an experiment and camped out in the library; now he's moved on to how quickly organs fail, how they're cost prohibitive, how you need to put a price on human life because otherwise you can't insure it. He's fingering bindings and tracing letters with his longest finger.

Bodies thaw. Your father's home becomes a sandbox where some cousin's daughter has been paid to take all the coats and topple them into an unused annex. Your aunt, the one who's notorious for forgetting her coat places, is going to leave her coat and come back to see if someone else left a better one worth taking. Her body's a frieze, she has tattooed a story of argonauts finding isles of women, isles of feathers and ichor, each island a body part. So you've heard. So many sons of gods on one boat in the center of her exposed clavicle.

You smell food being prepared and think, *it's too early*. Who's in the kitchen? Why did you insist on lox when he's not even here to eat his favorite food? It might be his mother, your grand, who will be cooking on her deathbed with a Bunsen burner on her lap. Eighty-nine and yet to cry about his passing. She hasn't left the kitchen; you know she won't. It skipped your father, but you inherited her instinct to exist as smally as possible.

You've taken off work for three days. Bereavement. You could have had ten days. Three. Ten. There doesn't seem to be much difference and using numbers seems insensitive. You have to put a number on bereavement for the productivity of your job. What do you do again? You work in a hospital, and you hate telling people that because they always want to know if you are a doctor.

One of his brothers brings bouquets of flowers, scentless. He drops them on your father's desk turned reception table in their cellophane, expecting someone else to arrange them, find a vase for them, and tell people *he* was the one who brought them. He doesn't greet you because he doesn't see you because you've managed to make it look like the door you are braced against needs a doorstop. You are facing a couch occupied by some of the greats who managed to make the journey to a house they've never seen except in old new year's cards when the three of you were still a family unit. They don't know you are his daughter because they don't see that well, and you are only pretending to be a part of their conversation so no one else sequesters your attention.

I got here first and salvaged my father from amongst his possessions. I've removed the third of seven Matryoshka dolls: the only one painted blue, ripped his favorite stories from two collections. In my car I have a handmade mug, the clay underside engraved with an *A*. A cerulean cashmere sweater that used to be much darker. A smooth flat river stone he always carried to help him think. Three cacti and his heat lamp.

Shortly after my father's funeral, the buzzards have taken what they wanted of him. I inventory the house, interested to see if what they wanted fit with what he cared about. My mother is here, sitting on a couch that wouldn't fit out the front door, two of his brothers settled for practically unused tools from the shed. They seemed upset. She hasn't been in this house for seven years and she refused to take anything of his even when they divorced. She didn't even ask about the mug with the *A* that she had made for his fortieth birthday.

"I watched them divide the watch collection," she says.

"Who?" I ask. She doesn't answer because it doesn't matter.

"And his collection of rugs and carpets."

A watch and rug collection divided, all the things he had brought together spread back across zip codes for some future collector to spend their life reamassing. Feathers remain of my relatives. Black feathers, dirty dishes, newly stained tablecloths. Without the mirrors, the house seems a little darker, a little smaller. Without some of the larger furnishings, the house seems a little bigger. So it might balance out to about the same size as before. Books have been picked through for their bindings, for their gilt and faux; nothing lovingly read was touched. Would he be happy about that?

I'll spend the night if the guest bed and linens haven't been taken. I light a menorah because the candleholders have been uncollected. My mother and I head to the kitchen to scrape food from dishes to trash can. We are both hungry. My grandmother is finally crying in the kitchen, putting away the dishes no one wanted because they couldn't tell whether the bucolic settings were hand-drawn in Japan or mass-produced in China. There is a horse dragging itself through a flooded rice field and a man trawling in its wake. Maybe people just don't want to be reminded of Monday.

ZAUN

Hiking, you say *we're lost* on a single-track

(Potency magic at our finger-slips not yet adept at conjuring, at dreaming the sumthings when some things we haven't seen, so chained by our actions and bond-aging crow's feet oh flights neverlanding o'er salt-pan or ocean our desertion at the center our eyeslit preservation a camel a cowlick of sand curling wavelets, combing for figurettes and summoning falcons and (sigh))

That a third a way up the trail (hallucinate a hammock) I stop smelling honeysuckle though it professes

(I forget thyself; the masks the hooks and the hold me at ransoms, at stakes battered ramparts and banners affections parades everyday til they lose all their grandeur amazement and stilted-acrobatics trapped-easy by welkin the lures dangling catch wrists swing netless and (sigh) that children keep shedding their dazzle they're pulling deflated balloons they're leaking their glitter and melt through the streets keep our muscles our meat salted-sugar rushed sleep poised for (sigh) I widen)

Aid stations with views I refuse, (a wind, a coughing: follows), waiting for the heights of the summit

(Attending beheadings and headings and beings attentive to (sigh) It's chaos, mashing our feelings and staring at Gorgons need solvents need portents and walls all a dooring their opens and closes their purpose their surface their gaps birthed from quarries from rubble restructured and goldleaf the ruptures not holding infusions or (sigh))

The cairn guiding our way above the tree line, (drips, skin
a chewed paper), allowing this substitution of stone

*(Inspired by oxygen a Triassic prison, verdant as living a frisson a
(sigh) its no wonder no vision no (sigh) a strongholding out armaments in
prayer holey in service of wonder of rain bows and arrows the shadows
of dragons in clouds from a steam trained by dresses wedding keys locks
and nesses all treasured with promise and promise in promise of ballads
of grapes all fermenting our torrents our fortune dam-captured waters keep
spawning the frog-croaks and grove-roosted ink-birds and song-swans and
heroes and herons much lighter than (sigh))*

(Air-thinner) where even the cairn path disappears on the
last (breath-catch) scramble to the summit

*(Much lighter than feathers the cranes building skyscrapers that live
for a thousand the years just mirroring skies,)*

The sense of (C's March, a tolling deep within) accom-
plishment lasting but a second

*((sigh) whiting to graying then bluing as emeralds look murky look
virulent they're sparkling clairvoyance invisible features from mephitic fissures a deep-set i'mperfection tongue-polished gums cupping pearls and
knuckles grown wiser from (sigh) from (sigh))*

There's a hawk circling in the sky below us

*(Heave hold me and load me in canons fuse-lit and nervous ours curvy
fruitions, lub me, make land to me stormmy beacheads-tailspun from the
salvos they're streaking there fumaroles here volleys come comets 'tween
castles afloating; buoyant our fires our warrings our hearth-smothered waters the waters a hearting; inundations a warming a warning awarding a
warbling from battened down hatchlings their mouths all in unison just
miming the feeding to come)*

Below us!, and still somehow I

IQA

المنهل Al Manhal, 허니버터칩, HARIBO, DORITOS 해오징어 Roasted Hot Squid, POM STICK Sour Cream, SPARE Pear Fruit Crisps, Crystal Geyser Natural Alpine Spring Water, New Jordan's Low-Sugar Granola, Ponky Puff Snacks, PediaSure, 北海鳕鱼香丝, Nic Nacs, alaçam, Merries エアスルー, Erikli, Святой источник, 高坑牛肉乾 KOW KUN BEEF JERKY, evian, 田辺農園のこだわりバナナ, Κορπή Φυσικό Μεταλλικό Νερό, DOLE, Al Ghadeer Water مياة الغدير, 칸쵸 초코, RETORNÁVEL Fanta, COFFEE-MATE, Palawat SMART WATER, Tropicana, DOUBLEMINT, FIJI, Knorr, DANONE, nutella, 고구마깡, samba, شيبسي بلايز, بطعم الطماطم والفلفل الحار, Freyma's Snack Beef & Chili.

Some flakes are so precious, delicate, egos tipping with bravado, fluent in grace and pulverization, worn, storm-tattered banners with the remnant pictures of the crests they made for themselves, that lemming fall, canyon edge those flakes getting a sniff of the updraft nine thousand leagues to the bottom, to get close enough to grab one you have to scoop your breath, hold it there like a kitten before it squirms, like hope it won't blow off in the microscopic breeze her hand generates moving toward it, a butterfly-effect wind: a hurricane somewhere in St. Kitts, wherever that is, and if he finally connects fingers to diaphanous flake— an entity bereaved of color in such a way it blinks in and out of this world with all of its chromatic assignations—we will think, now I will know what you feel like,

like the dust of butterfly wings, the cessation of want, sleep; but there is nothing in her fingers except residue, polyethylene smears, microscopic, immaterial, disintegrated and.

"Don't waste your time on the small stuff," Nurul Syasha tells Iqa. "You should know that by now."

Iqa's fingers are dusted.

"You think any of this garbage could have been Sheila Majid's?" Nurul Syasha follows up in Iqa's silence.

"Someone that famous doesn't use plastic," says Danish. "She's environmentally friendly."

"I hope you're right," says Nurul Syasha.

"Another European shipment," Nurul Syasha laughs, holding up a Poland Spring bottle.

"Poland Spring is an *American* company, from the state of Maine, founded in 1845," Danish informs the trio.

"It was only a joke, Danish. You've told us this before," Nurul Syasha scowls. "And you only know that because it's written on the label and you can read English."

"Iqa, did you eat today?" asks Nurul Syasha.

"Leave her be," says Danish.

"I'm just looking out for her. You're not her husband. And besides, she can nod."

Iqa nods to show she can. And Iqa can lie. Iqa can see Iqa's reflection in the filmy inside of a bag of Super Rings: hair baked and curly with dirt. Eyes reclaimed earthenware embracing deep fissures repaired with dribbles of gold. lashes, lids: curators. The grimy blemishes her skin brandishes: a knight's armor, dragon-fire camouflage for the way Iqa oxidizes even the immiscible: sheltered, caved, hermetic: our emotions from practice. Iqa only ever a shower away from destroying their world with her radiance; Danish pines; Nurul Syasha pines. When he exists in Iqa's eyes, when she sees herself trapped there within Iqa's fractures of gold, the revenant we, respire, cataclysms of life, dilations, tender immolations.

Iqa tosses the Super Ring bag, still tinted bilious with cheese, into her large trawling net. Could have been Sheila Majid's Super Ring bag, who knows? Danish might. Danish stores more info than Iqa and Nurul Syasha combined, except maybe for when it comes to celebrities; Nurul Syasha knows a lot about celebrities. And Iqa. What does Iqa know in her quiet?

"*Cik, cik,*" a young girl calls to Iqa, tugging on the back of her net. Iqa turns to face the small child, nearly thigh deep in plastic.

"What do you want, child?" Danish asks.

"I'm talking to *cik*, Uncle."

"Who are you calling *Uncle?*"

The girl sticks her tongue out.

"*Cik. Pretty miss.* Just a few ringgits."

"Does she look like she has a few ringgits?" demands Nurul Syasha. "Don't give her anything, Iqa."

"But you gave my brother ten ringgits yesterday."

"She did no such thing!" says Danish. "Now run off."

The girl gives Iqa one more pleading look; look returnal.

We took hundreds of millions of years to accomplish lungs. Fright came before we could even gasp for breath. To-day's horoscope: *We enjoy hard work and enjoy taking breaks.* To-night, the stars align around a Leo's roar behind clouds and a quiet moon; The Perseids crying muffled light down on a disappointment of gazers who had been convinced to leave their fabrications for a larger lullaby.

"Iqa, you are staying with Danish tonight. Danish, don't," Nurul Syasha cuts herself short. She trusts him. It's Iqa's quiet that stirs her to create words in the dead space. Kudzu-thick poise cascades from Iqa; it would only take a *single word*: for us to hang on for another thousand years, sonorous bell germinating seeds in the subterrane of their stomachs, a note always on the cusp of being sensed again.

"Iqa, I'm sorry about tonight. It's only one night," Nurul Syasha says. There are tears in her eyes and she hugs Iqa.

"*It's only one night*," Danish repeats, slightly offended by the display.

"I know. But we've been together for, what, eight months now, Iqa?"

Iqa shakes her head. Then nods twice in an upward direction.

"Longer? Yeah, almost a year now then. I wish we had seasons to count by."

"We have two. Monsoon season and monsoon season!" laughs Danish.

"You know what I mean! I'm going to buy a watch one of these days."

"Or maybe even a cell phone?" suggests Danish.

"Don't make fun of me, Danish. I'm going to have money. Speaking of which, Iqa, do you want me to cash in your plastic for the day?"

Iqa shrugs.

"You know you need money to buy food. I may not be around forever, *pretty miss*."

Iqa purses her lips into a kiss and Danish blushes.

"Okay, then. Goodbye you two. Meet you in the usual place tomorrow morning."

"Good luck at the clinic tonight," says Danish.

Iqa reaches out and embraces Nurul Syasha. Pigment diffusion. An artist sleeps a final stroke to canvas, a mixture of onyx, burnt umber, sepia, insinuating the shadow of gauntness in her subject's cheekbones. Iqa pulls away and touches Nurul Syasha's inflamed lymph nodes. Eye contact. They're reaching toward it; in these moments they can nearly taste what a tectonic influence the devastation of language would have born from the vocal folds of Iqa. Iqa's harmonics. We all shudder.

Nurul Syasha cries efficiently; experienced at cauterizing.

Danish's apartment slumps on crutches, a meter off the marshy loam, siding soggy and bailing paint in a slow waterfall like melting glass. Six or seven handmade steps, made with stripped siding-planks, lead up to a front door swollen and ebbing against its frame.

"I'd avoid the third and sixth step," Danish looks back at Iqa to get a sense of what she thinks of his living situation. "I'm going to fix them."

Iqa shrugs and it puts Danish at ease.

The entranceway groans and slackens with the freedom of the door's dislodging. Danish can't get the door back in place once he and Iqa are inside and he has to kick it for it to finally accept its counterpart.

"I'm going to get more furniture," Danish explains, looking at the floor table and pile of cushions. "I'm sorry about the," Danish starts. Iqa touches his shoulder. His eyes close.

Sun-warmed stones for lizards, reef-nooks and the protection of color and tides and the serenity of sea grass swaying patches of refracted shade, burrows, oaks, eggshell, shallows, your five tiny fingers finding the warmth of maternal skin. To live where dust gathers. Rafters, belfries: where do bats gather if not our stomachs? Steeples. Turrets. Lightning rods. Imaginary fish with the heads of tigers warding off fire. Call upon water: another monsoon season. Warding song of voodoo: broken CDs encoded with a music that will never play. She mimics the volume of our sun. A pitch he can't hear. But someone somewhere needed a miracle so badly as to birth song. Rhythms of sunshine and parched skin. Grandmother's quince jam recipe. The protectors we draw on our walls for our futures to find. Our kindness: thin spider silk lines refracting dew. It won't rain tomorrow.

"I'll start dinner," Danish says after that merciful infinity.

Danish goes overboard in his preparations, wanting to impress Iqa as much as he wants Nurul Syasha to know he made enough food to constitute a proper dinner. He even makes the canned fish he had been saving.

He watches Iqa eat for signs of praise or disappointment. She smiles. She eats all her food though it must be more than she's used to.

All dinner and after, Danish avoids the necessary conversation: there is only one bed in his quarters.

"Iqa," Danish begins explaining.

Iqa undresses. Thighs and stomach impossibly as tan as her face. Danish stares at her dark areole, then down to the tuft of hair that reminds him of underwear and then of her nakedness.

"Sorry. I didn't mean to. I've never seen . . . " Danish starts, before stopping even more embarrassed.

She motions for Danish to do the same but he can't bring himself to remove anything so she picks up her shirt off of the floor and puts it back on despite the humidity of the evening. The moon shatters across the clouds like a floodlight's afterglow, bathing Danish and Iqa gray. Sleep comes for Danish once Iqa's breathing provides a soft metronome to rhythm against.

Nurul Syasha isn't at the meeting spot the following morning.

"We should go to the clinic and see if Nurul Syasha is still there," Danish tells Iqa.

Nurul is on one of many thin mattresses skeltered out across the lounge-like waiting room, a dozen or so people sending out imperceptible signals for haste. She beams upon seeing Iqa and Danish.

"Sorry I couldn't meet up this morning. I would have lost my spot. I'm next," she explains.

"You haven't seen the doctor yet?" Danish asks. "It's been all night."

"I was able to sleep."

"We would have brought you food. I," Danish begins to explain the meal he cooked, but doesn't want to make Nurul Syasha feel as though she's been left out.

"That's okay. The clinic receives donations. I actually ate more than usual."

Danish is relieved that Nurul Syasha is in good spirits.

"We'll wait here with you. Then, when you are done, we can all leave together."

"I don't know how long it will be. Besides, you should be out making money," Nurul Syasha says back to Danish. They both look at Iqa, as though she might settle their dispute.

Little sediments of sedimentary, igneous, metamorphic imprisoned within blinds of sun-refracted mica, nothing in response: with what purpose does the tulip harness the bee to repeat their joint journey, stationary, flighty, archaic and gifted in the form of a pause, the forsworn pollen an intermediary, a simile for love. *Mistake not the pain of hunger, for we are empty* and *full, no less than the sum of all we yearn to be amaranthine.*

Danish looks to Nurul Syasha for mercy. *Just allow us to stay. Say that it's all right,* his eyes plead. Nurul, arbiter of clairvoyance, reads Danish and sides. Sighs.

"Actually, why don't you guys stay for the day. They've got a TV here. Plays the weather station mainly, but it's something to do."

"*record heat,*" someone bleats from a box above their heads. It is this announcement that brings forth the Danish and the Nurul Syasha from within themselves. And supposing Iqa stays within ourself.

"Good day to be inside," Danish says, but he is eyeing the others who wait in their own silent booths of thought, and instead of an open airy waiting lounge his eyes graze over the banks of fog our individual minds lose ourselves in like partitions, only to be interrupted by the occasional child who, unattuned to the subtle melodies of suffering, wails about hungers, wants, tireds, and tediums with tails as long as rats that nobody bothers to do anything about.

"I think I'm next," Nurul Syasha says, excitement creeping into her voice. "See that large guy who just went in?"

"Stained T-shirt?" Danish smirks, and some of the fog clears around them.

"That's the one. Well, I got here just after him. Tried to sign my forms quick but he's faster than he looks." Nurul Syasha. A smile.

Nurul Syasha is gone for longer than she intoned before her departure. But she was getting her wait-time's worth. Thirteen hours for two in the chamber.

She comes out pale but smiling. Iqa doesn't let on, taking in Nurul Syasha's pain and giving back the radiance of what Nurul Syasha thought she was projecting.

Danish sees into something. His mind flits with a phantasmagoria of plastic labels: 제주 삼다수, ACQUA PANNA Natural Spring Water, Crystal Geyser Natural Alpine Spring Water, Natural Mineral Water BUXTON, Cachantun ORIGINAL NATURAL Gasificada, Erikli, Arrowhead 100% Mountain Spring Water, evian, い・ろ・は・す 天然水 Natural Mineral Water, Κορπή Φυσικό Μεταλλικό Νερό, Al Ghadeer Water مياة الغدير, SMART WATER, FIJI, DANONE, Poland Spring 1845.

Everywhere on earth secret fonts; Nurul Syasha's next words, "Doctor gave me the all clear."

The effervescence of her words: every. single. one. popping. Something that wasn't falling ten minutes ago is falling. Nurul Syasha has trouble walking, words hidden terminal within her. She gives what she can't say, embracing both Danish and Iqa, pulling necks together and cheeks pressed in kiss. Danish wills his strength into Nurul Syasha. Iqa offers her face as long Nurul Syasha is prepared to keep it.

She tries her best not to cry until they are outside, the plumes of cars and calls of advertisements are betrayals to the solemness of what Nurul Syasha has learned. *But*, she thinks, but the thought doesn't move beyond that.

But at least, yes, the world still hums to itself.

But at least I can be forgotten. No.

But at least I'm still right here, right now, breathing in unison with my two best friends.

And then, on a sidewalk polluted with vendors, overripe fruit, body odor, color-washed buildings trying on whatever bleached patterns the sun foists upon them, honks of goose-necked car-people craning at the vehicle ahead just for a sniff of their place in the future, a laughing and solitary poodle-woman backpacking her dog and earphoning her conversation, rabbled clumpings of people pigeons rodents fire-backed ants aggregated into respectives based solely on communication, Iqa speaks.

Iqa's voice spreads in a suffused fretwork, our cerebral aurora, subterranean mycelial synapses that spate and calve, farther, kinesis outstretching the candescent, ebullient zephyrs braiding the welkin willing the pollen of our austral evolutions to root in the soil of glaciers, fluorine bogs, gold silver and blood pheasants, spittle, hydrothermal crabs, a boreal woman beset with the shame of forgetting her sister's birthday, every day a birth-day, pelagic tears freed from mother ocean in an evaporative blooming where breath upon breath, soft warm whispers from within blankets form the calm heart of moisture's calcifications, clouds weaving a basinet, a gale-nestled warm heat—reactions, chains, reactions lightning's fractals hunting and weakened, its movements a series of dead-ends in an invisible labyrinth until its flaxen hair rolls earthward from a deep purple quiver, an embrace, the rich rot of feathering moss and translucent fungal caps decomposing fallen worlds, once kissed by lightning, a warm breath, zephyred sisters hemispheres away on the same sun-faded sofa silent in the instant of us all, our Iqa, our golden filigree lacing our failures into exquisite equations, tracing gently our fractures, pewter, bronze, mercury, iron, all nearly seraphic in their transformation, as are we: a single point of light for less than the time it takes the human heart to respond to its own distant trumpet.

It, existence, the universe, the mind infinity, how we puzzle into place, how we are tiny reactors of unthought, oh, what potential lies there, the elusive fish depthed within the lake: rumored, fabulous, buoyed low and pushing water back and forth with a tail momentous as an osmium pendulum heavy-slow-devastating-undisturbing even the water it harmonizes through, and through, it is sunk there like a truth:

"Shhhh," rushes the wind. At once the boom of chaos of will of innateness.

"Shhhh," concur the cicada. The incandescence of an eye closing.

"Shhhh," infer the lips.

PAN

Prefix

-pan—(Greek πᾶν, pan, "all," "of everything")

Mythology

-Pan—god of the wild; the modern word "panic" is de-
rived from this

Astronomy

-Pan (moon)—a moon of Saturn

-Pan (crater)—on Amalthea, Jupiter's moon

Chemistry

-peroxyacyl nitrates (PAN)—irritants found in smog

Geology

-dry lake (or pan)—an ephemeral water body contained in
a shallow, flat basin

Geography

-Mount Pan—Ji Country, Tianjin, China

Zoology

-bonobo (Pan paniscus)—ape species known for its peace-
fulness; endangered

-common chimp (Pan troglodytes)—the other species
making up the Pan genus

Food and Drink

-pan—a type of cookware

Fiction

-Pan (novel)—by [1]Knut Hamsun, who gifted his Nobel Prize to Joseph Goebbels

-Peter Pan (character)—created by James Barrie. Originally from the 1902 novel *The Little White Bird*, adapted for the theater as the *Boy Who Wouldn't Grow Up*

Music

-pan pipes—instrument (also pan flute, as depicted with Pan (god))

Other

-pan-pan—distress call similar but weaker than Mayday

-drain pan

Lost Boys (disambiguation)

-1995

Overhead a quartet of Alpine swifts was returning to Africa from Europe—which did they consider home? Manifesting our collective jealousy, Natali zinged a rock, missing. Unspoken, we all felt better. We resented their eleven-thousand-kilometer journey on unobstructed highway, catching food as easily as one contracts malaria, their ability to sleep mid-flight—lulled by air currents, drafts and crosswinds—and how they collected moisture effortlessly in their beaks far above us and our Africa.

I heard they can fly for two hundred days nonstop, Fara said, the oldest at twelve.

I heard they can lay eggs and catch them while flying, joked Natali.

And they build traveling nests with scraps the wind kicks up, added Deesum, catching on.

I heard they never land, I said, but the mood had shifted as a jeep was heard distantly crushing and kicking out stone. We scanned our surroundings for underbrush, and even though I had become as thin as the swaying grass, it wasn't tall enough in the dry season to conceal us.

Our reluctance to be sheltered by thorn patches didn't delay us for long. The stonecrusher approached, branded with the Sudan People's Liberation Army's flag, offering food and homes for the conscripted. If it weren't for them raiding our villages for volunteers while we herded cattle or fetched water, taking Fara's father's hand when he refused to join before moving on to their next thought, to their next village, leaving him with the pain of a missing hand, a pain that would probably mature over decades of inability, leaving Deesum to return only to blood, and leaving me speculate as to the reason why my small village was completely empty when I came back with the water, I would have joined.

We aimed for Ethiopia, which shared a long border with Sudan, but even with a thousand kilometers of leeway, the border wasn't a finish line we could see, because while we walked animals hunted people hunted the world kept spinning sunsets, and after we turned our heads and bodies to speak to one another, or to avoid carrion that attracted so much more than us, or to pee, to sleep, to cry away from the others, we had to once again feel for the direction within us that we had lost.

The Boy Who Wouldn't Grow Up (disambiguation)
    -2001

Ambiguous loss:

When I wake to a caulking of clouds that have squeezed the sun down to what feels like four or five p.m., like my entire day has gone somewhere before I've had a chance to live it, where is the morning? Without my mother to make her flattened bean bread or my father to scold my laziness even when I'm up before him having already fetched water and gathered sticks, where is the morning? When they could be on the same continent as me, healthy, alive, or dead: to my oblivion, where is the mourning?

I was resettled here three years ago, and the flat expanses of Nebraska make me wonder if Americans think this is what Sudan was to us. But I have to be grateful. I have to work hard for things I don't care about. I eat fast food because it's more delicious than my mother's bean paste and it saddens me to know something tastier. I drive a car, my faucet runs—even when I don't want it to. I habitually catch drops in a pan and when I wake in the morning I see my reflection in the water, filled, so I dump it down the drain.

There's a room in my Nebraskan apartment with a door that's been locked since I've moved in. My landlord hasn't mentioned it, and my attempts to ask have been met with feigned confusion, or an attempt at avoidance which is indirectly blamed on my poor English. There is no keyhole and the door is of a solid wood that, when knocked on, doesn't resound with the hollow echo of cheaper materials. When I strain against its oakiness, I can hear a soft music that's been muffled to a pleasant murmuring, like parents talking or the landing of planes from the faraway near-sleep of my days spent in an Egyptian airport. That door once gave me a splinter, proving to me it's from somewhere in the way that I'm from somewhere, a splinter large enough to leave a hole when exhumed.

The Little White Bird (disambiguation)

-1958, The Four Pests Campaign, China

Vigilant with regards to rats, flies, mosquitoes, and sparrows. It used to be that a fly's frail coil snapped with the innocuous regularity of blinking, which puts into perspective how a single human death affects the pervading billions on this planet, or to point out how I once viewed through a fat telescope belonging to my father the hush-hush of a star closing its eye, and though its final candescence would have extinguished our entire galaxy, he set me with the impossible task of pointing out its particular darkness in the night sky the following night.

Up until two years ago, flies and mosquitoes died their familiar, uncredited deaths without being tallied at the end of the month. I've since personally shoveled kilograms of them onto the scales to be weighed, recorded, reported, and then publicly broadcasted amidst delphic complements about our progress. I myself don't understand a kilogram of flies even after having seen what it looks like. Even as a "public official" (now in name only), I don't understand the progress I'm reporting and am not smart enough to explain how the death of a fly brings glory to China.

This morning I tarry through the village with a fresh limp, staining the rising sun with my inefficacy. A group of energetic Red Guards, who should be in school instead of on patrol, reminded me of my white uniform's vestigiality by pushing me into the dirt.

Shabby furnaces annexing family homes cause me to temporarily forget the desiccated rice fields. Though the people of this village have less reason to rise with the sun now that China is an industrializing nation, a few are tending to their metallurgy as they used to their fertile rice beds. There's Chzen Yao, Chu Win, Lao Yung, all of whom prefer to watch the smoke tarnish a blue sky than meet my eyes, and my name hasn't been spoken in greeting in so long I sometimes forget I have one. My constitutional ends later than usual back at the maw of my father's former rice field and the boon of my tardiness is that children are already playing.

The boys chase the sparrows from tree to tree, and occasionally chase the girls who also chase the sparrows from tree to tree, using pots and pans, rocks and scree, wings a fever, panic and glee, hair ribbons crimsoning my vision; they don't know where to go, anger-terror simultaneous, unable to land, their nests destroyed along with any hopes of eggs, any hopes of resettling, and they smear the sky with their mortality. And at some point, while they futilely push through a leaden sky, one of the birds, having exhausted everything—a sight that I never would have believed if I hadn't seen it twenty-two months ago and hundreds of times since – falls.

Neverland (disambiguation)
  -July, 1920
  Jimmy couldn't see the world around him at age eight, so intensely focused he was on baseball and overcoming his failures. After games I'd make him a special dinner which he'd eat with the guilt of a retired soldier receiving a war medal. He didn't just want to hit a home run, he embodied the struggle:

practicing his swing in his room when it rained, doing push-ups, asking for dumbbells—can you imagine it, an eight-year-old lifting weights in a white tank top and pajama bottoms? He reminds me so much of my father, his grandfather, who, even after two heart attacks wouldn't stop his morning exercise regimen. But Jimmy's gifts resided elsewhere and I told him so, though I knew he wouldn't be swayed. No one in class thinks science is great, Momom, he said to me. But I still encouraged him on both fronts, bought him those dumbbells though always reminding him, homework first. After about four months' time, his bat cracked that ball and the white streak surged for outer space—but he was a small child, straining to lift those dumbbells, spilling water down his shirt as he gulped from hard work, often saying things like, We need to do our best every day, huh Momom, often wincing at the pitch, looking braver before the next one—

-August, 1945 et al.

[1]*I believe I can read a little in the souls of those around me*; maybe it is not so . . . We sit in a room and I seem to see what's going on in the hearts of these people. Maybe it is not so . . .

Jimmy Only shivered, despite August. The room was cold, a feeling amplified by the cushionless metal chair that, because of his thin summer suit, seemed to touch his skin directly. It comforted him to hear everyone expressing a unified discontent.

A bomber plodded along the Pacific toward Japan's southern coast while those at US headquarters gathered around the radio transmitter. Only recounted how many years he had worked at splitting atoms, and then how many more it took to put that discovery into practice. So many scientists and engineers from all over the world had gathered in Los Alamos among other US sites to offer their minds to this task; creating something to end the war.

What can I recall of the chaos the world has been bathed in these past years? And for playing such an integral role, how can I feel so . . . Only searched for the word, untouched? He had anticipated these negative thoughts; in fact, all the scientists of the Manhattan Project had prepared for them. They were inalienable consequences of their work, the minor by-products of the peace they hoped to proliferate.

As if on cue, two officers began a conversation about the armistice that would ensue from their collective endeavor.

"It damn well better," Dr. Oppenheimer added, which made everyone laugh. The radio static broke to the chatter of the bomber pilots as they spotted the Japanese mainland for the first time. Excitement followed. A few scientists worried about what would happen if the bomb didn't go off. An officer remarked, "Well, it's still as heavy as anything I've ever seen!" But Jimmy Only wasn't listening. He was lost inside fractions of possibility. How many people could I have been? He remembered the conversation with Albert Einstein that ended up facilitating the Manhattan Project. He swam back even further into his mind, to when he was discovering fission—a warm smile burning his face. And if I had become those different people, would someone have become me?

Despite his meanderings, Jimmy Only was proud of what they had created, and prouder still of everyone's reluctance to have done so. The severity had been lost on no one; tiny conversations and worried countenances that assured him of their collective good flooded his consciousness.

The static broke again, "We are closing in on target A."

Hiroshima.

Only looked around at all the prominent figures and thought, Will all of us ever be in a room together again? He was suddenly aware of being a part of History with a capital H. In this enormous moment he was connected to his brothers in the room in a way he had never felt before. They all hung there in the same gravity.

"Are we ending the war or continuing it perpetually?" a colleague of his said in a whisper so soft that Only wondered whether or not it had been said at all. He scanned the faces of scientists and soldiers for who could have disrupted his introspection.

"We're releasing the payload," patched through.

Seconds passed.

The static was muffled by an intense silence.

Only's ears screamed with the lack of sound and the passing seconds stretched so thin that he could see between them entire lives—past, present and future—unfolding, ending, and their brilliant phoenixes:

A young girl named Ziri goes to school for the first time today in Angola, nearly floating down the dirt path that takes her to the unknown. In one life she becomes an astronaut, in another a biologist, in a third a carpenter, a zoologist; and in all of them she becomes a teacher, unaware as she runs home from school to share her life with her mother that she already is one.

Greece's rocky coast has just been obliterated by an asteroid that had been pulled into the earth's stratosphere. Galênê wants to be the first one to explore the site but her mother won't let her go. Decades later, her mother contracts cancer and Galênê visits for the first time in a long while, noticing the cracks in her mother's skin crafted from so many thousands of smiles, causing Galênê to touch her own smooth face as if to remind herself of those times she had refused to smile back. How that stoicism had seemed so triumphant. She smiles sadly at her own stupidity and it matures into something more once she's moved past it, gazing at the woman who gave her so much more than the life she couldn't see she had, savoring the cracks her face creates, silently dubbing them, love for mother, hoping that they'll remain after the smile has faded.

An elderly woman teaches her granddaughter the few words of Aramaic that have been passed down to her. The young girl asks why they speak Arabic in Oman now but the grandmother doesn't have an answer. The words sound foreign and precious to the young girl so she is careful with them.

The daughter of a Japanese farmer touches piano keys and creates a world. Her younger sister applauds, not yet awake to the full brilliance of her creation. When she is eighteen and studying in England, the younger remembers that brief nocturne for some reason when she is having sex for the first time. And it's often the ghost of that melody that wakes her from those lapses in consciousness that happen while driving, times when the mind becomes so transparent that it melds with the world.

A ballerina is giving what she knows will be the last performance of her career and her parents and siblings have come all the way from St. Petersburg to see it. She receives a special mention as the performers bow. Her father is standing along with the rest of the audience; he takes breaks during his applause to wipe his eyes. She has never seen him do this.

And for some reason during those infinite seconds Only thought of his own life, his mother playing baseball with him, how badly he wanted to hit a home run, and that one time, watching the ball sailing over the heads of the basemen and into the outfield, how it fell with an unspectacular thud in the grass.

He had tears in his eyes now; how he wished it would never land.

ACKNOWLEDGMENTS

Thank you to Ray Levy for finding this manuscript. To my mom, a lifelong reader and font of encouragement. For my sister, Nicole, a source of inspiration. To Daniel Waterman, you are a lighthouse; thank you for guiding me through the process. To FC2, for your belief and for inviting me into the collective. To Ben Sklar, for random bits of everything throughout my entire life. To Tim Parrish for years of encouragement. To Lily Davenport for the careful edit. And for MoMa.

Story Acknowledgements:
Lan Caihe, dedicated to Ray Levy.
Jimmy Only, dedicated to Jefferson Schultz. You must understand abduction has its effect on people. *Most biographical information on Mr. Only was taken from the interview: *Only at Home* between Jimmy Only and Jefferson Schultz.
Iqa, for IQA.
Баба, dedicated to kate garnett, without whom so many of the stories in this collection wouldn't exist.
Paolo and Nic., dedicated to my sister, Nicole.
Graciela, por los defensores del bosque y la mariposa Monarca.
Delia, dedicated to curious Delia and Quora members Paul Stockley, Thomas Perkins, Trevor Ray Slone, and Theresa Atkins.
akiko for Yosano Akiko.

Low-Risk Activities, dedicated to Edna B. Foa.
Ness, for Ness Fererjo, thank you for sharing your diary.
Zaun, for Michelle Z.
pan, in loving memory of Natali Angok يرحمه الله.

www.ingramcontent.com/pod-product-compliance
Lightning Source LLC
Chambersburg PA
CBHW070648100726
47907CB00007B/2145